A Mountie from ... cracking cop from ... when these two get together . . . *hide*.

All The Queen's Horses is the fourth novel in the Due South series. Other titles include:

#1 *Death In The Wilderness*
#2 *An Invitation To Romance*
#3 *Vaulting North*

due SOUTH

ALL THE QUEEN'S HORSES

Tom McGregor

B■XTREE

First published in 1997 by Boxtree
an imprint of Macmillan Publishers Ltd,
25 Eccleston Place, London, SW1W 9NF
and Basingstoke

Associated companies throughout the world

© 1997 Alliance Communications Corporation in Trust.
Licensed by Copyright Promotions Ltd.

ISBN 0 7522 2259 7

All rights reserved. No part of this publication may be reproduced, stored in or introduced into a retrieval system, or transmitted, in any form, or by any means (electronic, mechanical, photocopying, recording or otherwise) without the prior written permission of the publisher. Any person who does any unauthorized act in relation to this publication may be liable to criminal prosecution and civil claims for damage.

Cover design by Shoot That Tiger!

Cover photographs by Michael Courtney
Adapted from the original stories *All the Queen's Horses* by Paul Gross, John Krizanc and Paul Quarrington, teleplay by Paul Gross, and *Red, White or Blue* by Paul Gross and John Krizanc, teleplay by Paul Gross.
Based on the television series *due*South™, an Alliance Communications Corporation Production

9 8 7 6 5 4 3 2 1

A CIP catalogue record for this book is available from
the British Library

Typeset in Sabon by SX Composing DTP, Rayleigh, Essex
Printed and bound in Great Britain by
Mackays of Chatham plc, Kent

This book is sold subject to the condition that it shall not, by way of trade or otherwise, be lent, resold, hired out, or otherwise circulated without the publisher's prior consent in any form of binding or cover other than that in which it is published and without a similar condition being imposed upon a subsequent purchaser.

PART ONE

Prologue

'Fraser?'

'Yes, sir?'

'We need to improve our image.'

'Sir?' Benton Fraser stared, pu[zzled at the] woman in front of him.

'Our image, Fraser.' Superinten[dent Thatcher] stared back. Her face, as usual, was [an inscrutable] mask. 'The image of the Royal Cana[dian Mounted] Police.'

Resplendent in his dress uniform [of red tunic and] blue trousers, Benton drew himself up to his full height. 'I wasn't aware there was anything wrong with our image, sir.' He sounded piqued, insulted. Paramount to him was the image he reflected, not for the greater good of himself, but for that of the Mounties.

Thatcher (for obvious reasons she rarely divulged her christian name) looked down for a moment. Didn't he know, she thought? Wasn't he aware that his presence, in the shape of six-foot two of gorgeous hunkdom, unnerved her? No, she corrected herself, of course he didn't. She had, in the two months since she had taken over as

Canadian Consul in Chicago, gone to great lengths to conceal her feelings for Constable Benton Fraser. Such had been her inner turmoil that she had, at first, tried to fire him. At the time, he had been convinced that – personal feelings aside – she had ample grounds for doing so.

Both Thatcher and Benton now preferred to draw a veil over the firing episode, attributing it to an inauspicious first encounter. Thatcher had been appointed while Benton was in Canada on a holiday – a holiday that, Benton-like, had involved a hijacking, a plane-crash, temporary blindness, paralysis, dehydration and a near-fatal plunge down a waterfall. The nature of that holiday was not unrelated to his boss's decision to put him on probation when he returned after three weeks' recuperation. And the probation was, in turn, not unrelated to Benton becoming involved in a bank robbery which had resulted, as these things do, with the Royal Canadian Mounted Police being sued for post traumatic stress by the thwarted robbers. Benton had been under the impression that his role in thwarting the robbers would see an end to his probation. He was spot on there: Superintendent Thatcher fired him.

Ray Vecchio, detective with the Chicago Police Department and Benton's best friend, told him Thatcher's actions were illegal. 'She cannot,' he had declared with authority, 'just get rid of you like that.'

'She just did, Ray.'

'How long have you been . . . what is it . . . doorman at the Consulate?'

'Sentry, Ray. And I am not a sentry. I am the Deputy Chief Liaison Officer for the Royal Canadian Mounted Police in Chicago.'

'Well there you go then. She's not even your real boss. You're a civil servant, Benny. She can't just get rid of you like that.'

Relieved, Benton had gone back to the Consulate and related this piece of information to Thatcher. She had stared at him from under her long, unnerving dark lashes. 'Fine,' she had said, after a long silence. 'Then you'll just have to make things easy for me by requesting a transfer.' As she had uttered the words, she had crossed her fingers under the desk and hoped against hope that the authorities in Ottawa would refuse the transfer. They did.

Since then, neither of them had referred to the episode. Now they enjoyed a healthy working relationship; Thatcher lusted quietly beneath her brittle facade while Benton, to his professional discomfiture, became increasingly hot under the restrictive collar of his dress uniform whenever he found himself in Thatcher's presence for more than a few minutes.

Refocussing her attention on the matter in hand, quelling a moment of quiet lust, Thatcher looked up at her deputy. 'Where were we?' she demanded.

Benton forced his thoughts away from his collar and back to the matter in hand. 'We were discussing our image, sir.'

'Ah. Yes. I am not,' continued Thatcher, 'referring to your image in particular, Fraser. I'm concerned about the Mounties in general; about the way the public perceives us. Especially the American public.'

'Oh.' Thatcher, thought Benton, was full of surprises. Why, having bulldozed her way through the ranks, terrorizing Ottawa and now Chicago with her utter ruthlessness, was she now concerned about image? Wasn't she aware of how most people perceived *her*? The Iron Lady; Attila the Nun? Didn't she know that she had singlehandedly rekindled the centuries-old antipathy between Americans and Canadians? It was, thought Benton, a shame that such a good-looking woman – with, he was increasingly beginning to suspect, a soft heart – should present such a hard, threatening image. There was, he knew, a Real Human Being under the brittle exterior. Three times now, when she had thought he wasn't looking, he had caught her smiling at him. It was almost enough to make him forgive her for trying to fire him. Thank goodness, he thought, the powers that be in Ottawa had thwarted her. Thank goodness they had declared that being sued by the bank robbers for post traumatic stress syndrome did not constitute ample grounds for his dismissal.

Aware that he was staring dumbly at his senior officer, Benton shook himself out of his reverie. 'Uh ... and what do you propose we do about our image ... sir?'

Thatcher hoped Benton couldn't see the corners of her mouth twitching. She had to admit that the 'sir' business – quite unconscious on Benton's part – gave her a certain frisson. Anyway, she preferred it to the correct alternative: there was something horribly hard and sexless about the word 'ma'am'. 'I propose, Fraser, that we make a television programme about the history of the Royal Canadian Mounted Police; an informative and edifying documentary for the benefit of the American people.'

'Ah.'

'Is that all you can say, Fraser?'

'No, sir. Well, that is to say ...'

'Dismissed.'

'Understood.' Benton inclined his head in a semblance of a bow and then turned to leave the room. He wasn't remotely perturbed by what others might have seen as an abrupt dismissal. It was just Thatcher's way. She seemed, for some odd reason, to go all peculiar after a few minutes in his presence.

Thatcher breathed a sigh of relief as Benton closed the door behind him. She blamed America for the change that had come over her in recent months. On too many occasions, she had almost let her guard down, had been in danger of revealing her true inner feelings. Shaking her head, she rummaged in her top drawer for her glasses (she never wore them in front of Benton). Perhaps, she reflected, I'm under stress. Then she dismissed the thought as rapidly as she had dismissed Benton. Stress, in Canada, was something that you learned about in geology classes; something that happened to the layers of the earth's crust as they pressed against each other. She was not, she reminded herself, a crust.

But as she tried to concentrate on the paperwork in front of her, she couldn't banish the thought that she had become, to some extent, an American. Was this programme idea really about boosting the image of the Mounties abroad? Or was it something altogether different: was it Thatcher trying to secure her fifteen minutes of fame by appearing on the small screen? Whatever the real reason, it was too late to rethink or abandon the idea. In the hyper-efficient and diligent manner she had acquired since coming to America, Thatcher had already set the wheels in motion for the making of the documentary.

Chapter One

Beaming with pride, Benton leaned against the train and watched the spectacle being enacted in front of him. This, he thought, was magnificent: this was what being a Mountie was all about. Comradeship, honour, skill and dedication. Admittedly, there was no longer much call for riding horses in the famous circular formation, battle lances at the ready, but it still made for an impressive sight. Not for the first time since their arrival in Southern Manitoba, Benton silently congratulated Thatcher on her impeccable organization.

With full and wholehearted approval from Ottawa and with backing of nationwide TV stations in both Canada and the States, Thatcher was about to make history – silencing those who had prayed fervently and often that Thatcher herself would become history before too long. The programme was going to be broadcast from coast to coast: the image of the Royal Canadian Mounted Police would be boosted far and wide. No longer would cynics call the Mounties antique supermen in silly hats. No: instead they would marvel at the extraordinary levels of equestrian skill and marvel at the sight of the Mounties – forty of them in total – who had congregated to take part in the documentary.

Less marvellous, thought Benton (but being Benton he kept these thoughts to himself) was the production team making the documentary. To him, they appeared affected and superficial, more 'actory' than actors – and desperately pleased with themselves. The director with the beret and the clipboard, for instance, seemed to be more of a thespian than a technician; his whole bearing screamed 'auteur'.

Unseen by Benton, that same director – who rejoiced in the suspicious name of Robert Bolt – was replaying rough cuts of the morning's shooting to Thatcher. The footage, of thirty-two Mounties enacting their famed musical ride against the stunning backdrop of the plains of Southern Manitoba, was accompanied by narration for the benefit of those – i.e. everyone in the world – who were unfamiliar with the subject matter. 'The musical ride,' announced the gravelly voice, 'was performed by the Royal Canadian Mounted Police as a showcase of their prodigious skill in horsemanship.'

'Amazing,' said Bolt.

Thatcher shot him a suspicious look. He was, she correctly surmised, complimenting his own direction abilities rather than the hugely impressive dressage skills of the Mounties. Furthermore, he hadn't once complimented Thatcher on her own skills: on the not inconsiderable feat of seeing that everything ran like clockwork during the breaks in filming and, more importantly, of marshalling her men and her horses on and off the specially-chartered train that was taking them from one location to another. The fact that Benton was largely responsible for all the organization was, to Thatcher, a detail so minor as to be irrelevant.

Yet what really bothered her about Bolt was that he had developed a nasty habit of ignoring her. Like now, for instance. He had returned to the monitor and was nodding again in appreciation of his own filming prowess. 'The thirty-two riders,' continued the narrator, 'the thirty-two horses, the scarlet tunic, the battle lance and the precision drills which culminate in the 'dome' formation . . .'

'Chicago,' drooled Bolt, 'is going to love this . . .'

' . . . have inspired wonder since their inception in 1873. Theirs is a history rich in tradition, and the musical ride has secured its place as an enduring symbol of a nation.'

Thatcher thought that was just a tad over the top, but Bolt had no such reservations. 'This,' he said as he turned to her, 'is to the bone beautiful. Now we need close-ups. Faces. Boom, boom, boom. Faces, we need faces.'

Rather pointedly, Thatcher patted her newly-washed hair and presented Bolt with a close-up of her own delectable face. 'You don't think,' she suggested disingenuously, 'we need, say, an "on the spot" interview?'

'You kidding?' Bolt was horrified. 'You mean one of those Seventies "let's-talk-about-what-we-already-know" interviews? I don't think so.' He wagged a disapproving, directorial finger at Thatcher. 'What America wants is inspiration, not chit-chat. America,' he finished, 'wants heroes.' Then he turned away from Thatcher to continue with his own heroic endeavour.

Feeling rather foolish and not a little angry, Thatcher cast around for someone else to speak to. The only person in the near vicinity who wasn't rushing around being arty was Benton and he, she noted with disapproval, was lounging against the side of a train carriage, talking to himself. Typical, she thought with a sudden stab of wounded pride; he rarely says more than a word to me, but he can chat animatedly to himself. She stalked off in the opposite direction, forgetting that the main reason for the lack of happy, chatty intercourse between her and Benton was because she invariably opened their conversations with the word 'dismissed'.

There was much that Thatcher didn't know about Benton. She didn't know that he had lost his mother when he was six. She wasn't aware that his quixotic personality had much to do with being raised by his maternal grandparents (librarians, both) in small towns in the inhospitable Northwest Territories while his Mountie father pursued Mountie affairs in even more inhospitable locations. She didn't know that those grandparents had died (of disappointment) shortly after Benton himself had followed in his father's footsteps at the age of eighteen. Nor did she know that his father had been murdered two years previously and that Benton and Ray Vecchio had brought his murderer to justice, thereby cementing a strong, if volatile friendship.

But the most peculiar piece of information about Benton to which she was not privy was that when he appeared to be talking to himself he was, in fact, conversing with his father.

Benton had long since ceased to be surprised when his father appeared by his side. He had also given up trying to work out whether that appearance was in his mind, in his father's mind, in both, in the ether, or for real. All he knew was that when his late parent popped up, he was visible only to Benton and that he would dispense a great deal of useless advice to his only child.

Robert Fraser saw things differently. His guilt at being a largely absent parent had manifested itself only when he was dead as well as absent – a problem whichever way you looked at it. The dead part didn't bother Robert too much. There were, he conceded, many advantages to being deceased, the principle one being that you couldn't be killed.

Now that he had more time on his hands, Robert was becoming increasingly aware of the fact that he hadn't been a particularly diligent parent. His role, as he now saw it, was to watch over his son and protect him from the evils of the modern world. This he did by dispensing useful advice.

On this particular occasion, however, Robert's appearance was purely for social reasons.

'Nothing quite like it, is there, Son?' he said as, smiling delightedly, he took in the activity in front of him.

'Oh, hi, Dad.' Benton turned and smiled at his father. He was, he noted, dressed for the occasion in his pristine scarlet and blue uniform. 'I didn't know you were coming.'

'Wouldn't have missed it for the world. Stirs the blood.'

'You don't have blood,' sighed Benton. 'You're dead.' It wasn't, he felt, a criticism – his father didn't take too kindly to critics – just a factual observation.

But lack of blood, to Robert, was but a minor detail. He shrugged and tapped his chest. 'I've got the memory of blood. Something's beating in there. Hey!' he suddenly exclaimed as one of the Mounties detached himself from the group in front of them. 'Would you look at that? My old stable mate!'

Benton looked. The man, slightly wizened,

completely grey, was indeed familiar. He wore the slightly puzzled yet contented smile of someone who was pleasantly surprised that he was still alive.

'Yes,' said Benton. 'Sergeant Frobisher and I had a long talk yesterday. He was telling me about the time you spent together in Moosejaw. I must say,' he added, 'he looks good, doesn't he?'

That was the wrong thing to say. His father shot him a suspicious and not altogether friendly glance and, on the defensive, claimed that it was 'just the uniform'.

Benton shrugged. 'Well, why don't you go say hello?'

Suddenly shy, Robert seemed to shrink into himself. 'Nah. I wouldn't want to impose.'

'But you're dead. It's not really an imposition.'

'Well,' replied his father, obviously tempted but a little wary, 'I don't know if I'd be able to.'

'What do you mean?' Benton turned and frowned at his parent. 'Oh, I see. You mean he might not see you because . . .'

'. . . because I'm dead.'

'Well,' said Benton with another shrug. 'You could give it a try.'

But then Frobisher himself saw Benton and, with a smile of recognition, dismounted and walked over to him. 'Ah, Benton! Good to see you.' Then, grinning, he waved the cane he was carrying. 'Have they given you one of these yet?'

'Er . . . not yet sir, no.'

'Well, you're young.' With a rueful smile, he patted his right thigh. 'In a few years time that steel blade you took in the leg will catch up with you, just like it did me.'

Given that he had never fallen victim to a steel blade, Benton thought that was highly unlikely but, polite as ever, refrained from saying so.

His good manners were called upon again a moment later as Frobisher fell prey to a loud and lengthy attack of gas. Benton pretended not to notice. Beside him, however, his father wrinkled his nose in disgust. 'Try spending a week,' he said, wincing at the memory, 'on a stakeout in Dead Horse Gulch with *that*.'

'Do you mind?' said Benton, offended for the other man.

'What?' said Frobisher.

'Nothing, sir.'

'Oh.' Then, seeing that his fellow riders were dismounting and leading their horses into the train, Frobisher gestured with his cane. 'Seems like they're loading up. Shall we?' Without waiting for Benton, he marched off back to his horse.

'You coming?' Benton whispered to his father as Frobisher forged ahead.

'No son. Never was a fan of train travel myself. Anyway,' he added with the smug smile that only the deceased can muster, 'I have my own methods of transport.' Head held high and whistling a jaunty jingle, he disappeared.

'You know,' said Frobisher, as Benton caught up with him at the train steps, 'the boys introduced me to a real eye-opener the other night. Moose hock rolled in wild boar tongue,' he recalled with relish, 'covered with gorgonzola cheese.'

Sounds perfectly revolting, thought Benton. 'I'd like to try that sometime,' he lied.

Frobisher wagged a cautionary finger. 'Don't be too hasty. It seems,' he added, as another volley of gas erupted from his nether regions, 'to follow you around for a while.'

Thank goodness, thought Benton as he hauled himself into the train after the unfragrant Frobisher, that the filming was nearly finished. Barring any mishaps, they would be back in Chicago by tomorrow.

But mishaps, in Benton's world, had a terrible habit of happening. Today was going to prove to be no exception.

Still miffed about Bolt's cavalier treatment of her, Thatcher was determined to re-establish her role as the ultimate authoritarian. As soon as the Mounties were settled and the train in motion, she began to stride up and down the carriage, casting menacing looks at anyone unwise enough to meet her eye. Clad entirely in black, stilettoes pounding the floor and shoulder pads swaying from side to side, she resembled a monochrome Cruella de Vil.

'We will speak,' she said as she paced, 'only when we are spoken to. We will keep our responses short and to the point. We will maintain our postures. Above all,' she finished as each and every Mountie quaked with fear, 'we will act naturally.'

An unnatural silence descended as Thatcher reached Benton at the far end of the carriage. 'Why,' she whispered, 'are they staring like that?'

Benton looked at the glazed expressions. 'I expect,' he said, 'that they're terrified, sir.'

Ridiculous, thought Thatcher. How were the film crew supposed to film this bunch of corpses? How, more to the point, would it look on film if her happy band of men stared at her like rabbits caught in the headlights of the sort of deadly vehicle that took no hostages? 'The whole point of this exercise,' she sighed, 'is to bring a new dynamism to our image. Look at them!' she snapped as she pointed with a long red talon, 'They're stiffs! Make them do something, Fraser. Anything. They can break into song for all I care. They just can't sit there.'

'Into song?'

'Yes.' Suddenly pleased with the idea, Thatcher nodded. 'Yes. Make them sing.'

'Understood.' Benton too was pleased. He was fond of singing. Even Ray had said he had a good voice, a compliment devalued by the fact Ray was tone deaf, but a compliment nonetheless.

By way of one of those neatly contrived coincidences that need no explanation, the Mountie closest to Benton had a guitar at his feet. Benton gestured to it. 'May I?'

The Mountie, too terrified to open his mouth in Thatcher's presence, merely nodded.

'Thank you kindly.' Benton picked up the instrument. Then, smiling happily to himself, he strummed a few chords and, in a move that brought smiles to the faces of every other Mountie in the carriage, he began to play 'Ride Forever'. Soon the carriage was filled with the lusty and surprisingly tuneful sound of forty Mounties belting out their much-loved anthem.

Thatcher was delighted; so much so that the tiniest hint of a smile flickered briefly on her lips. Yet the smile remained a hint, a hopeful and tentative suggestion. Realizing it was trying to flower on the wrong face, it gave up and fled.

After a moment, Thatcher realized that Bolt was standing behind her and turned to him with a suggestion of her own: that he film her as she listened to the singing. She had already decided on the correct half-wistful, half-admiring expression she would wear. It would, she knew, convey the impression of a professional dedicated to her work yet who was not so aloof that she was incapable of enjoying herself with her troops. 'Mucking in'; that was it.

Bolt, however, had other ideas. Most of them revolved around the career in which he moonlighted when he wasn't directing films. This career was robbery. Hitherto, Bolt had been less successful in that line of work than he had been in directing (and he wasn't exactly renowned for the latter). Now all that was about to change. He and his accomplices had a plan that simply couldn't fail. He knew this because the plan had been largely devised by his much more intelligent and criminally successful brother. The train and its forty-odd Mountie passengers (some of whom appeared very odd indeed) was now heading home to Chicago. The crew of that train would very soon be tied up; the Mounties would be gassed and unconscious, and Bolt and his fellow partners in crime would be in control of the train and its occupants and in a position to issue their demands to the outside world.

Those demands were not modest. Ten million dollars to be deposited in an unnamed account by the City of Chicago or else the runaway train and its hostages would hurtle into Chicago Central Police Station, brakes disarmed, and the explosives on board would be programmed to detonate at exactly the same time as the train entered the station at a hundred miles an hour. It was all perfectly simple: the best piece of direction Bolt had ever planned. His only regrets were that it wouldn't be filmed and, of course, that the plan wasn't actually his. Yet the cessation in filming had its compensations. The wretched woman, for instance, who was at this moment batting her eyelids at the camera, was wasting her time. There was no film in the camera; there was no cable connecting the boom to the sound recordist; there was, in short, no point in the hard-nosed harridan pouting into the lens. Soon she, like the other Mounties, would be sound asleep.

As he pointed the empty camera at Benton, Bolt looked up to the roof of the carriage. The air conditioning ducts, if Georgie Racine had done his work properly, would soon be belching forth invisible but potent gas that would silence the Mounties for a good few hours. And a good thing too, thought Bolt. This hearty 'Ride Forever' business was beginning to get to him.

In front of him, Benton's relaxed expression gave way to a frown as he continued strumming his guitar. Something, his intuition told him, was not quite right. The camera crew all looked as if they were waiting for something to happen. And weren't those footsteps he could hear on the roof? And why, he thought with a sudden stab of fear, wasn't the camera wired-up for sound? It was the last realization that galvanized him into action. Instead of launching lustily into the second verse of the anthem, he handed the guitar back to its owner, stood up and walked towards Thatcher.

Thatcher herself was having a few problems – the least of which was Benton. Bolt was ignoring her. 'I think you'll find,' she said with icy hauteur, 'that with myself in the frame . . .'

'Not now, lady,' snapped Bolt. 'Can't you see I'm busy?'

Nobody, thought Thatcher, *nobody* speaks to me like that. She was in the process of composing a terrifying tirade of abuse when Benton appeared in front of her.

'Not now, Fraser,' she snapped. 'Can't you see I'm busy?'

But with a force that surprised her (and, if she were truthful, rendered her all a-quiver), Benton grabbed her by the elbow and pulled her towards the carriage door. To her even greater surprise, the crew's P.A. – a sulky little piece if ever Thatcher had seen one – tried to block their way. Only after a cautionary look from Bolt did she let them pass.

'Thank you kindly,' said Benton as he opened the door and ushered Thatcher into the caboose. Neither of them noticed that the P.A. locked the door behind them.

Indignant now that the moment of quivering had passed, Thatcher rounded on her deputy. 'Fraser,' she hissed, 'I was in the middle of a very important . . .'

To her surprise, Benton held up an authoritative

hand to silence her. 'And I apologize for interrupting, sir, but I believe something is amiss.'

'Oh. Well, I suppose there is always room for improvement. But on the whole I think we've got some promising voices here.'

'No, it's not with the singers, sir. It's with the film crew.'

'The film crew?'

'If indeed that is what they are.' As he spoke, Benton turned and looked through the glass door into the carriage. Bolt and his crew, suddenly frenetically busy, were now at the far end.

Thatcher, too, looked back. 'What do you suppose they're doing, Fraser?'

'Not filming, sir.' Stepping forward, Benton tried to open the door. 'And the fact that they've locked this door would indicate to me that they are intent on keeping the men together so that they can . . .'

'Can what?'

'I think,' said Benton as he watched the crew leave the carriage, 'they're going to do something to them.'

'What, Fraser?' Thatcher was becoming frantic. Nobody – except, of course, her good self – was allowed to interfere with her men.

'Listen,' commanded Benton.

Thatcher pressed her ear to the door. 'To what? I can't hear anything.'

'Exactly, sir. They've stopped singing.'

'So? Maybe they've finished the song.'

'I don't think so, sir. You see, it has several verses and . . .'

'I'm well aware of how many verses our anthem has, Fraser!' Anger, thought Thatcher, is the best defence against ignorance.

'Yes, sir. Sorry, sir. But in that case, why would they all suddenly fall asleep in the middle of the second verse?'

Again Thatcher peered into the cabin. Sure enough, every single Mountie was slumped against the back of his seat, mouth lolling open and eyes firmly closed. 'They've gassed them!' she spluttered.

'It would appear so, sir.'

But as they watched, an elderly Mountie at the rear of the cabin stood up, looked around in an embarrassed fashion, and made his way to the bathroom at his end of the cabin. This Mountie was Sergeant Buck Frobisher and his embarrassment was huge. Having produced so much gas of his own, he was strangely immune to the effects of the vapours belching out of the air-conditioning ducts. Worse, he was under the impression that the vapours were in fact belching from somewhere else and that it was he who had gassed his fellow Mounties. 'Ah, men,' he mumbled as he slunk down the aisle. 'I didn't realize . . . uh, sorry . . . I didn't know . . .' Crippled with embarrassment, he flung open the bathroom door and slammed it behind him, vowing never again to go anywhere near moose hock rolled in wild boar tongue covered with gorgonzola cheese.

'Well,' said Thatcher from behind the other door, 'what do you suppose we do?'

'I'd like a moment to think about that, sir.'

The moment, however, proved to be a short one. Before Thatcher had a chance to reply, Benton lunged sideways and threw himself out of the open window.

For another moment – one that resonated longer and with considerable shock – Thatcher remained rooted to the spot. Then, recovering her wits, she peered outwards and downwards. The train was speeding across a viaduct: below it was a gorge. Benton was nowhere in sight. 'Well,' sighed Thatcher. 'That's *very* helpful.' Then she withdrew from the window and pondered her options. That took yet another, much shorter moment: a moment that ended with a sigh of despair when she looked once more through to the carriage and saw Bolt and his cronies, handkerchiefs pressed to their mouths, running towards her. Most of her men were unconscious, one of them was in the bathroom, and the only one in whom she had any faith – although of course she would never admit this to him – had decided to jump ship, as it were. Her position was not good. Not good at all.

It was, in fact, better than she feared. While there were those (and they were legion) who reckoned Benton Fraser was certifiably insane, none of them would have imagined him mad enough to hurl himself out of a fast-moving train without good reason. And they would have been right. Benton's reason was, to Benton, perfectly sensible. A carriage-full of somnolent Mounties separated Thatcher and himself from the only other conscious member of their team. It was therefore essential to reach Frobisher and inform him of the position they were now in. And that was why Benton was pulling himself along the cables underneath the train towards the bathroom and its embarrassed occupant.

Time, thought Benton as he hauled himself past one deadly wheel after another, was of the essence. Not so much because of what Bolt and his cronies might do next, but because of Frobisher's imminent activities.

Benton sighed with relief when he reached the underside of the bathroom, identifiable by what he liked to think of as a waste disposal chute rather than the wrong end of the toilet bowl. 'Sergeant Frobisher?' he yelled up the chute. 'Before you continue, may I have a word with you?'

Above him, Frobisher's surprise was total. He was, in fact, beginning to think that he was hallucinating. Gassing a trainload of Mounties was – given the unhappy combination of moose, boar and gorgonzola – *just* believable: having company in a room this size was not. Still, best to be sure. He looked around and, failing to find the source of the voice, decided to play for time. 'Friend or foe?' he enquired.

'A friend, I assure you.'

Frobisher frowned. 'Where are you?'

'I'm right here, sir,' replied the disembodied voice.

Frobisher peered into the basin. 'In the sink?'

'No sir. To . . . er, to the rear.'

This, thought Frobisher, was ridiculous. Deeply suspicious of his own sanity, he peered down the toilet bowl. Then he experienced a sensation rare to people engaged in that activity: enormous relief. 'Great Scott,' he bellowed as he saw the familiar face. 'Benton!'

'I'm glad to see you're alright, sir.'

'Well, that's a matter of opinion,' replied Frobisher, thinking of the moose and the somewhat urgent reason for his being in this particular place at this particular time. 'What are you doing in my toilet?'

'I've come to debrief you, sir.'

How peculiar, thought Frobisher. 'Something wrong with the door?'

'We have a problem, sir,' shouted Benton up the chute. 'It is my belief that the men have all been gassed.'

So it *was* true, thought Frobisher. He sensed an unbecoming blush approaching. 'Oh my God,' he said, more to himself than to Benton.

'Yes, and furthermore, it is my belief that this train is no longer under our control.'

So, thought Frobisher with mounting horror, I've gassed the driver as well. 'It's worse than I thought,' he yelled back.

'Yes, sir, and I thought it prudent to inform you.'

'Inform me?' Frobisher nearly laughed. 'I've been living with it for a week.'

Benton hadn't a clue what the man was talking about. 'Sir . . .? I'm sorry, but I can't see how this relates to the terrorists.'

'Neither can I,' said Frobisher, who hadn't a clue what Benton was talking about.

Benton tried again. 'It is my belief that this train has been taken over by terrorists and that they have gassed the men into a stupor.'

Frobisher was delighted. 'Ah! Well, I must say, that's a relief!'

'A relief?' Benton was beginning to fear for Frobisher's sanity.

Frobisher, however, was revelling in the confirmation of that sanity. Suddenly businesslike, he leaned closer into the toilet bowl. 'How many terrorists?' he barked.

'Undetermined, sir.'

'Strategy?'

'Unformed. I thought,' continued Benton, 'I should first assess your status and then report back to our superior officer. In the meantime I suggest you just continue ... uh ... continue with your current, um ... project.' With that, he reached up through the chute to shake hands with Frobisher.

Although more than a little nonplussed by the sight, Frobisher, like Benton, was a stickler for good manners. Leaning down into the bowl, he reciprocated the gesture. 'Very well,' he said, shaking the proffered hand. 'Good luck, son.'

A firm, manly handshake and then Benton was gone: back the way he had come, seemingly oblivious to the dangers of dangling about underneath a train that was travelling at more than a hundred miles an hour.

Back in the bathroom, Frobisher was not so successful in his own purpose. His hand was now stuck. Try as he might, he couldn't wrench it free of the caress of the white porcelain. 'Uh ... Benton? Benton,' he repeated, his voice rising in panic. 'My arm is stuck!'

No reply.

'In the hole!' bellowed Frobisher. Then, refusing to entertain the thought that Benton had departed, he yelled even louder. 'Give me some help, Constable. That's an order!'

'God,' came the unexpected reply. 'You sound like an old man.'

So stunned was Frobisher that he didn't reply at first. Such a remark was so staggeringly un-Benton-like; such insubordination was unthinkable from Robert Fraser's son. 'I sound like a *what*?' he thundered.

'An old man.'

Again Frobisher didn't reply immediately. It was beginning to dawn on him that the voice was not Benton's. Furthermore, its source was not beneath him, but behind him. Fearing the worst, suspecting that one of the terrorists had broken into the bathroom to monitor his unorthodox ablutions, he wrenched once more and, purple-faced with the effort, managed to pull his hand free. 'Old man!' he shouted as he whirled round. 'I'll tell you something . . .'

But there the outrage ended and the words stuck in his mouth. Standing beside the basin, not two feet away from him, was Sergeant Robert Fraser, his very old – and very deceased – comrade in arms. He was smiling broadly and looking at Buck with a fondness he had never displayed in life. 'How are you, Buck?' he said, the smile now tinged with amusement as he registered the total shock on Frobisher's face.

The answer – yet to be articulated – was that Frobisher wasn't feeling too good. First there was the gas problem. Then there was the fact that he had nearly lost a hand. Added to that was the little matter of their being stuck on a fast-moving train at the mercy of an unknown number of terrorists with, as yet, no strategic plan of action designed to thwart them. And now there was a dead man standing in front of him. He must, after all, be hallucinating.

'Well,' said his old friend. 'Aren't you going to say anything?'

'. . . Bob?' At last Frobisher found his voice.

'Yes. It's me.'

'I am *not* an old man.'

Bob Fraser chuckled. 'Yes you are. You're sixty-seven. Same age as me.'

'But you're *dead*.'

Bob Fraser waved a dismissive hand. 'I know *that*. I was just trying to make you feel better about being old.'

'Eh?'

'Well,' said Bob. 'I died two years ago – when I was sixty-five. If I were still alive I'd be sixty-seven but I'm dead so technically I'm still sixty-five.'

'Why's that?'

'You don't age when you're dead.'

'No,' said Frobisher. 'I must say,' he added grudgingly, 'you're looking well on it.'

'Thank you.'

Then Frobisher blinked several times, scratched his head, closed his eyes for a full ten seconds and then opened them again. It was no use. Bob was still there. He took a deep breath and scrutinized the smiling apparition. 'I do not,' he said without much conviction, 'believe this.'

'Oh? What is there about this situation that you can't believe? That I'm dead?'

This time it was Frobisher who made the impatient, dismissive gesture. 'No, absolutely not. I believe you're dead. But there's one thing that bothers me. You seem to be who you seem to be. But by the same token,' he countered, wagging an accusatory finger, 'you do not seem to be who you do not seem to be. And that's a different story.' Looking immensely pleased with himself, he folded his arms across his chest. 'There you are.'

Poor Buck, thought Bob. Senile dementia was setting in. 'Alright,' he said. 'You want proof?'

'What?'

'Do you want proof?'

'Of what?'

'That I am who I say I am.'

'Absolutely. Proof. That's the thing. There we are.'

'Well, ask me a question then.'

'What?'

'No,' sighed Bob. 'Something more personal than that.'

'Oh . . . oh yes. I see what you mean.' For a moment Frobisher stared, unseeing, at the opposite wall. His attention was focused on another decade, another place, another life. 'Very well,' he said at length. 'On April 23rd, 1957, sixty miles north of Destruction Bay, two men stood on a rope bridge which spanned a canyon.' Eyebrows raised, he looked at the other man. Bob merely nodded. 'On the other side of the bridge,' he continued, 'a woman was held in the clutches of a deviant. The two men had two cartridges between them, and one rifle. It was an impossible shot, but each one knew that whoever made that shot would be the man to secure the love of the woman. The first man,' he said in a now-wistful voice, 'tried and failed. The second man tried and . . . and he won the whole shooting match.' The hurt, he realized with a pang, was still there. Even after four decades. He cast a nasty little glance at Bob.

But Bob didn't notice. He, too, had been transported into the past. 'We were happy,' he sighed. 'Caroline and I.'

'Yeah, I know that. I know that. I know that.' Frobisher didn't care to dwell on the subject. 'But the question is,' he added, 'these two men, through their long years of friendship, often talked about that impossible shot. And when they did, what did they call it?'

'The shot, you mean?'

'Yes. The shot.'

'Well . . . the shot. They . . . they called it . . .'

Hah! thought Frobisher. An imposter after all.

'Time is up,' he announced with glee.

'Oh come on!'

'Bob Fraser would have given me the answer in one second.'

'Well, I'm dead,' wailed Bob. 'It affects your memory.'

Secure in his victory, Frobisher pointed at the door. 'Out,' he barked. 'Out. Now.'

'Alright! It was called . . .' Bob knew it was there, knew it lurked somewhere in his memory. If only . . . 'Yes!' he shouted suddenly. 'It was called "The Great Yukon Double Douglas Fir Spruce Telescoping Bank Shot".'

'My God! My God!' Frobisher's mouth fell open, revealing rather more denture than was currently modish. 'It's you! Bob Fraser!' Overcome with delight, he leaped forward to hug his old friend. The leap was an unfortunate move, resulting as it did in his forehead making heavy and sudden contact with the mirror on the opposite wall. Stars appeared in front of his eyes and then, as he turned, so did Bob. 'Oh,' he said, realizing. 'Does that always happen?'

Bob brushed the question aside, making a mental note to warn people, in future, about the non-material nature of his appearances. Benton, for instance, had fallen into a ditch the first time he had tried to hug him. I am, thought Bob with pride, like a precious object; you can look but you can't touch. 'That's not important,' he said to Buck as he brought his mind back to the present predicament. 'The important thing is you're in quite a pickle, my friend.' He looked Frobisher in the eye. 'You've got a train to stop.'

Frobisher nodded. 'Right you are. Er . . . how do you stop a train?'

Bob shook his head and quietly congratulated himself for defeating the ageing process. Those extra two years were really telling on Buck. 'You stop a train,' he said as he opened the door, 'by putting on the brakes. 'Come on.'

34

Chapter Two

Detective Ray Vecchio, poker player extraordinaire (his own description) was having a ball. Not only was he winning at poker, but he was having three days' holiday. Added to that (and as compensation should he begin to lose at poker) was the fact that Benton owed him a favour. A big favour. Benton had asked Ray to look after his pet wolf while he was on the three-day film shoot. Ray had replied that he would be delighted to help – but that he would have to take three days' holiday in order to do so. He had managed to justify this lie to himself on the grounds that excellence at poker demanded a facility for lying.

Diefenbaker, the wolf, had no objection to Ray's methods of animal-sitting. He was more than happy to sit by the poker players for three days on the trot, munching the endless plates of cheesy crispy things that Ray handed down to him. As far as he was concerned, it beat the hell out of chasing around Chicago on some hair-brained scheme of Benton's . . . or Ray's. Chicago was windy and cold and inhospitable to wolves and, more to the point, Dief was rather fed up with the trouble Benton and

Ray seemed to attract. Each, in his lupine opinion, was as bad as the other in that respect.

Ray didn't see things that way. It was beginning to occur to him that, because things had been quiet during Benton's absence, it must be Benton, not he, who had a penchant for attracting trouble – or at least for annoying other people. By 'other people' Ray, of course, meant Ray. The one phone call Ray had received from Benton since his departure seemed to confirm that theory. Benton had phoned from the train, claiming that Ray had instructed him to do so.

'I did not!' Ray had been adamant.

'Yes, you did, Ray,' had been Benton's equally certain response. 'In fact, your exact words were: "let me know how it goes".'

Ray had been obliged to call a temporary halt to the poker game in order to explain, in his most patient manner (Ray confused patience with condescension) what he had meant by the remark. 'You see,' he had sighed, reflecting on his good fortune to have been born an American and not a Canadian, 'this is another thing that's wrong with you, Benny. When somebody tells you to "let them know how it goes", they don't mean that you should call them and let them know how it goes as it's still going. What they mean is you should "let them know how it goes after it's all said and done and gone". You understand?'

'Not entirely, no,' had been Benton's response as he had reflected on his good fortune not to be American and therefore irate all the time. Then he had asked after Diefenbaker's health. Ray had responded, with total confidence, that the wolf had never been better. This, in fact, hadn't been strictly true. Diefenbaker was feeling slightly sick after so many cheesy crispy things – but then Ray hadn't known that. Being a wolf and therefore insatiably greedy, Dief, queasy or not, was reluctant to pass up on the offer of food. The memory of nearly starving to death during his infancy in the Northwest Territories remained with him. He actually felt it had warped him; turned him into a human being with a lapdog's longing for comfort, trapped in the body of a wolf. And even that body had its faults. Diefenbaker was deaf. Selectively and therefore selfishly deaf, but deaf nonetheless.

And now, a day after that first telephone call, Ray's telephone was ringing again. He knew beyond a shadow of a doubt that it was Benton because the only other people who knew his cellphone number, apart from his colleagues, were sitting round the table with him. And not even Ray's colleagues were crazy enough to phone him when he was on holiday. No, he sighed to himself, it had to be Benton. Only Benton would phone when Ray's hands were full of the cards with which he intended to scoop the massive pot on the table in front of them.

Not taking his eyes off the action at the table, Ray switched his cards to his left hand and grabbed the phone with his right. 'Look,' he growled into the mouthpiece, 'I'm holding the bullet in Low Chicago in a twelve hundred-dollar pot that keeps growing. This better be good.'

It was. Benton's voice, strangled and barely recognizable, articulated words that Ray, in the middle of the most potentially lucrative game of his life, really did not want to hear. 'This is Constable Benton Fraser of the Royal Canadian Mounted Police.' Benny, thought Ray as he upped the stakes on the table, sounds as if he's got a gun to his head. 'I am reading,' continued Benton, 'from a prepared text.'

Oh my God, thought Ray. He *has* got a gun to his head. With an anguished wail, he turned to address the other players. 'Am I some sort of God?' he shouted. 'Am I some sort of bad luck God?' The other players, who hadn't a clue what he was talking about but knew him for the excitable Italian-American he was, looked at each other and shrugged.

Do I listen to Benton, thought Ray in panic, or do I win twelve hundred dollars? There was no competition. 'Hold on!' he pleaded down the phone. Then he leaped up, grabbed his tape recorder from the mantelpiece, switched it on and banged it on to the poker table. Picking up the phone again, he yelled 'Okay! Shoot!' down the line and then slammed the phone on top of the recorder.

Benton's tones, muffled now and more surprised than anguished, wafted over to the poker players. His actual words, however, were drowned out by the frenzied resumption of the betting. 'We are on a charter train, coded 56023. It is travelling on the Palliser Line and is now held hostage. Any attempt to board the train will result in the death of those on board. Any sighting of aircraft will result in death. Any . . . uh, any attempt to . . .' totally nonplussed by the lack of response from Ray, Benton began to falter. Beside him, an equally puzzled Bolt leaned forward and grabbed the receiver. Playing for time, he said to himself. That was what the policeman must be doing at the other end. 'Our demands,' he barked down the phone, 'are as follows . . . Ten million dollars . . .' Pausing theatrically to let the enormity of the sum sink in, he was more than a little surprised by the reaction from the other end. The voice that he assumed was Detective Vecchio's responded with the words 'See you ten; raise you ten.'

Deciding that he had misheard, Bolt carried on. 'Ten million dollars, to be delivered by Detective First Grade Raymond Vecchio of the Chicago Police Department, *unaccompanied*, to station siding thirty three . . .'

'I'll see you that three hundred. Raise you a hundred.' The words, although barely audible to Bolt, deepened his astonishment. He was beginning to wonder if this Vecchio person was entirely sane. This was not, in his experience, the way to respond to a dire threat. 'Station siding thirty-three,' he repeated, 'on the Palliser Line, by four p.m. central standard time.' Then, just to emphasize to Vecchio that he meant business, he added a dire warning. 'Be ever vigilant, America, for the enemy is already among us.'

But Ray couldn't even hear the enemy. All he was aware of was the sound of his own voice as he let out a whoop of delight and gathered his winnings to his breast. Benton's dilemma was temporarily forgotten; the fate of forty hostages thundering through Illinois on a runaway train was consigned, for the moment, to his tape recorder. Ray was on a high; nothing and nobody was going to spoil his triumph. Not even Diefenbaker, who had heard every word (giving lie to his supposed deafness) and who was now whining at his feet, was going to spoil his triumph.

Back in the train, Bolt looked at Georgie Racine. Racine looked at Freya Chichester-Clark (not her real name), Production Assistant turned would-be assassin. She was standing behind Benton and Thatcher, waving a gun around. 'So,' she bellowed, 'what's with this Vecchio guy? Is he some kinda deaf mute or something?'

'No,' said Benton. As ever in times of stress, he appeared completely unruffled, totally at ease with himself and his surroundings. This was intensely annoying to Freya. Apart from the fact that the Mountie was supposed to be terrified, he was also required to find her irresistibly attractive. And here he was, showing no sign of either terror or lust. Worse, he was now casting a look of mild rebuke in her direction. He was offended, it appeared, for her criticism of the Chicago cop.

'So why,' snarled Freya, 'didn't he say anything?'

'I imagine he was just assimilating the information imparted down the phone whilst preparing to do as instructed.' Privately, Benton imagined no such thing. He had heard the clink of the poker chips, had realized that Ray had taped rather than listened to the phone call. And now he feared that Ray would be so elated by his win that he would forget to listen to the tape.

Still expressionless, Benton looked over to Thatcher. She, however, was enveloped in a simmering rage that had nothing to do with hostages, hijacking, ransom money and imminent death. She was furious that Bolt, not five minutes earlier, had instructed her to change into her Mountie dress uniform. 'I love a woman in uniform,' he had gloated. 'And in particular uniforms that are so darned arresting. Now get changed!'

Thatcher would sooner have died than change in front of a man who – in common with the careers of most of her ex-employees – was nasty, brutish and short. And then she had become aware of the gun pressed against her forehead and came to the conclusion that changing her attire was, after all, preferable to dying.

Her rage, however, had intensified over the past few minutes. It had nothing to do with Ray's cavalier attitude to their predicament, but with the fact that Freya was so clearly infatuated with Benton. Wasn't she aware that whatever passion lurked in Benton's breast was secretly, tortuously directed at herself? And besides, didn't the woman have any dignity? In Thatcher's book, it was a pretty poor sort of criminal who undressed her hostages with her eyes.

That last thought lifted her mood somewhat. She turned, haughty as ever, to Freya. 'I have every confidence,' she drawled, 'that Detective Vecchio will obey your . . . your orders.' The last word was accompanied by a supercilious curl of her lips; a suggestion that she would, were she less polite, have inserted the word 'little' before 'orders'.

Freya was momentarily taken aback – and showed it. Then she remembered her impressive, double-barrelled name and the double-barrelled shotgun in her left hand and felt happier. 'Well, lady,' she sneered. 'You'd better damn well hope and pray that he does obey. This train ain't going to stop for nothing or nobody until we get that money.'

But Freya had reckoned without Bob Fraser and Buck Frobisher. She could have been forgiven for the former: he was, after all, invisible to her and her colleagues. But all of them had forgotten about Frobisher, and were blissfully unaware that, accompanied by his deceased colleague, he was making his way to the engine of the train.

The driver had been unceremoniously ousted from his seat and knocked unconscious at the same time as the Mounties had been gassed. His place at the controls had been taken by one Frankie Moliere, ex-vision mixer to the film crew, now returned to his true vocation as a terrorist.

Moliere looked round as he heard the door open. Assuming that it was one of his colleagues, he was more than a little surprised to see an elderly Mountie standing in the doorway. 'Hey . . .!' he began, rising in anger to his feet.

But age had not withered the speed of Frobisher's reactions. Two things occurred to him simultaneously: one was that this man was smaller than he, the other was that the window in the engine room was wide open. Without pausing for breath, he sprang forward, lifted the outraged terrorist off his feet and threw him out of the window. 'Ah hah!' he crowed, as Moliere flew from the speeding train.

Bob Fraser, standing behind him, was less than enthusiastic. 'Hum,' was all he said.

Annoyed, Frobisher turned round to his deceased friend. 'What are you "humming" about? I just got rid of one of the enemy.'

Bob Fraser shrugged. 'Uh . . . nothing. It's nothing.'

Frobisher exhaled deeply, not, this time, from his nether regions. 'Well, when you humm, it always means something. So what's wrong?'

Bob gestured towards the controls in front of them. 'Well, do you know how to operate a train?'

'Er . . . I was counting on you.'

'I haven't the foggiest.'

'Oh.' Too late, Frobisher regretted the hasty violence with which he had despatched Moliere into the outside world. Then he saw the real driver huddled in the corner. 'Look! He'll know.'

'He's unconscious.'

'Oh. Well . . . .' Frowning, Frobisher looked around. 'Well . . . it can't be that hard. Must be someplace where they put the coal.'

'Buck,' sighed his friend, 'haven't you noticed that there's no smoke coming from this train?'

'Isn't there?' Buck brightened at the words. 'Well that's good, then. That means they must have run out of coal.'

'Er . . . no. There never was any coal.'

'What do you mean?'

'I mean,' said an increasingly exasperated Bob Fraser, 'that this isn't a *steam train*. It's not powered by coal. It runs on electricity.'

'Electricity? Good God.' Frobisher looked exceedingly disapproving. 'What next.' Then, again, he looked around. 'Well, there must be a plug somewhere . . .'

'No, Buck. No plugs. But there has to be a brake somewhere.'

'Ah! The brake! I knew there had to be something.' Happy again, Frobisher cast around for something resembling a mechanism that might stop the train. Yet, like his friend, he was totally unfamiliar with any sort of engine, least of all that of a train, and his face was creased with doubt as he rummaged around amongst the bewildering array of dials and switches that populated the little cabin.

Eventually – and to his delight – it was he, not Bob, who found it. 'Ah hah!' he said, not for the first time.

'What have you got there?' Bob looked suspiciously at his crouching friend.

'I've found it. I've found the "brake"!'

Like a child beaten by a rival in a treasure hunt, Bob shot a darkly mutinous look at the victor. Why wasn't he, possessed as he was with all the unearthly powers of the dead, the one to find the brake? Where were all those powers of extra-sensory perception that the living insisted belonged to the dead? Not in the engine-room of this particular train, that was for sure.

Frowning, Bob crouched down beside his friend. 'What,' he asked loftily, 'makes you think it's the brake?'

'It's written right on it.' Frobisher pointed to the red lever. 'See . . . it says "brake".'

But Bob was unimpressed. 'It could be a ruse.'

Well aware that his friend was just plain jealous at not finding it first, Frobisher was equally scathing. 'And exactly to what end would that be a ruse?'

'Something criminal.'

'Are you insinuating,' sighed Frobisher, 'that an entire design crew deliberately mis-labelled key elements of a train?'

'It's possible.'

Death, thought Frobisher, does strange things to people. Bob had never been the brightest of men, but now his brain seemed positively pickled. 'I'm talking,' he said as he shook his head, 'to a lunatic.'

But as far as Bob was concerned, Frobisher was the lunatic. 'Now, you see,' he continued, 'this is what's wrong with you, Buck. You discount everything but the probable. It's why,' he added with gleeful malice, 'you didn't make that shot way back then.'

Frobisher bit back an equally cutting reply. Don't get riled, he told himself. If you're not allowed to speak ill of the dead, then you shouldn't speak ill *to* them either. 'Don't think,' he said after a moment, 'you can twist the knife, Bob. That was springtime. I had my allergies. My eyes were cloudy. Anyway,' he added, not wishing to pursue the subject, 'this *is* the brake, and I'm going to bring this train to a halt.'

Bob held out a restraining hand. 'Wait. Wait!'

'What?'

Bob pointed to two suspiciously new-looking wires beneath the lever. 'What are these?'

'Wires,' said Frobisher with an uninterested shrug. Then, following his friend's gaze, he saw that the wires stretched back towards the body of the train – and that the brake lever itself was loose. Alarm bells ringing in his mind, he gave the lever a tentative pull. Nothing happened. 'Oh my God,' he said as he turned, horrified, to face Bob. 'They've bypassed the brakes.'

His mouth set in a grim, thin line, Bob grunted and pulled himself upright. 'We'd better get hold of Benton. This train,' he finished in doom-laden tones, 'is a runaway.'

'This train,' repeated Frobisher as the enormity of the situation sank in, 'is a runaway.'

Chapter Three

Ray was not one to disappoint his friends. Apart from the fact that he was anyway in danger of losing three of them (the losers at poker had not been gracious), he was well aware that a friend in need was a friend indeed. And he needed Benton: the Mountie owed him a favour and would hardly be in a position to repay it if he were dead. Furthermore, as Ray told a worried Diefenbaker, he was a policeman – a senior policeman at that – and was not going to pass up the opportunity of becoming even more senior by thwarting one of the most spectacular attempts at extortion he had yet encountered.

So, as soon as his friends had taken their somewhat grumpy leave, Ray played back the tape of Benton's phone call. And as soon as he had done that, he headed, Diefenbaker in tow, for the police station. His colleagues, he knew, were about to get the shock of their lives. They would sooner have bet on the imminence of a blue moon than on Ray appearing at work when he was officially on holiday.

Commander Welsh, Chief of the Precinct,

experienced something more akin to disappointment than shock when Ray burst through the door. Why, he said to himself as he watched him approach, did he have this sneaking suspicion that Vecchio was not here to say a cheery 'hello'; to pass the time of day with his colleagues? Even when the detective was officially 'at work', his presence in the building invariably made Welsh feel uneasy. The word Vecchio, he knew, meant old in Italian; so why was it Welsh who felt old whenever the other man approached? At least this time there was some sort of small compensation: he wasn't accompanied by the Mountie. Ray on his own usually meant trouble – but with the Mountie in tow that trouble had a capital T and was preceded by Big.

But when Ray charged into his office, looking not just serious but *worried*, Welsh's heart sank. And when Ray played the tape to him, that organ all but dropped to his boots. One Mountie on his patch had been bad enough. Now, suddenly, he seemed to be responsible for a trainload of them. The fact that they were hostages and in grave danger didn't worry him unduly. What upset him was that the train was heading full-tilt towards Chicago; *his* city. And what caused him grave concern was that whatever ignorant terrorist had hatched the plan in the first place seemed to be intent on shooting himself in the foot. Why else would he have stipulated that Detective Raymond

Vecchio deliver the ransom money?

Ray stood expectantly at the other side of the desk, awaiting Welsh's response. Desperately concerned, he was also strangely elated. This would be the biggest operation he had ever worked on – and he was going to be in charge.

Welsh, when at last he spoke, had a different view of the situation. 'Vecchio?'

'Sir?'

'Get the FBI.'

Two hours later, Ray was still fuming. What did the FBI have that he hadn't got? Sure, they had fancy names and poncey headquarters in Quantico, Virginia – but as far as Ray was concerned they were too consumed by their own importance to focus on the things that really mattered. And one of the things that really mattered was, of course, Ray.

Ray looked on in disgust at the agents who had turned one of the interview rooms at the station into what they called a 'Situation Room'. They had installed a complicated computer on the desk and were all rushing around being important and wearing headphones; but what had they actually achieved? Nothing. Precisely nothing.

The one who styled himself as Agent Ford suddenly broke off from a frenzied conversation with his portable phone and barked an order. 'Agent Deeter!'

'Sir?'

'Into the Commander's room. We now have a strategy. And you,' he added to Ray, 'better come too.'

Ray was sorely tempted to protest at the disparaging tone that had accompanied the word 'you' – and at the eyebrows that beetled along in an insulting fashion across Ford's brow. Yet somehow Ford's expression didn't invite an outraged response. Feeling less than proud of himself, Ray followed Agent Deeter down the corridor to Welsh's office.

If Welsh was irritated at the way Ford had taken command of the situation, he didn't show it. In truth, he *was* annoyed by Ford's manner, but reckoned it was less of a cross to bear than Vecchio's incompetence. And anyway, there was another, more professional reason for tolerating Ford's behaviour: if the train blew up along with its Mountie cargo and half of Chicago, then the FBI, not the Chicago PD, would take the blame. That, as far as Welsh was concerned, was incentive enough for allowing Ford to pace around his office – as he was doing now – playing God.

'Alright gentlemen!' announced Ford as he paced. 'Here is our situation: representatives from State National Security Council are meeting regarding the larger implications of the situation. As I speak, two Rapid Response Teams are flying in from Fort Bragg and Quantico . . .'

But that was too much for Ray. Before he could check himself, his mouth opened in a mocking manner, allowing a snide little remark to slip out. 'What?' he sneered. 'No B-52 Squadron?'

Ford rounded on him, impelled by the full fury of the FBI. 'You have a problem with this, Detective?'

Ray held the other man's gaze. 'Well, you know, Ford. We all have our own style. Me?' he added, pointing to his chest. 'If I got a sore head, I don't take a chainsaw to it – I swallow a couple of aspirin.'

'Vecchio!' snapped Welsh with a nod towards Ford. 'This is their field protocol.'

'Lieutenant,' said Ray. 'There are people on that train. Sure,' he added with a token towards humanity, 'they're Canadians, but they're still people. And we don't know what their situation is.'

'Precisely, Detective. We can't talk to them, so we don't know. Therefore,' continued Ford with a withering look, 'we assume the situation has gone sour until we receive confirmation one way or the other. And let's be clear about one thing, Detective Vecchio. You're a conduit – you deliver the money, nothing more. Do we understand each other?'

The corner of Welsh's mouth twitched as Ray made an equally withering reply. 'No. I don't think that's possible.'

Thankfully, Agent Deeter broke the hostile

silence. Gesturing to the piece of paper he had been reading, he looked up, frowning, at Welsh. 'I don't understand. This here says the Mounties were being filmed doing a musical ride. What is a musical ride? Some kind of theme park thing?'

'Ah!' said Welsh. 'No, no, no.' A dreamy and, to Ray, totally unexpected look came into his eyes as he began his explanation. 'It's much more than that. It's thirty-two riders moving as one . . . perfect harmony between man and beast. A kaleidoscope of manes and tails and battle lances criss-crossing in a collage of synchronous movement.' Staring through unseeing eyes at the far wall, Welsh looked for a moment as if he were about to cry. 'It takes your breath away.'

It had taken Ray's breath away as well. What had happened to the list of unprintable expletives Welsh usually uttered when the word 'Mountie' was mentioned? Where the litany of abuse whenever Benton Fraser's name was mentioned? This was indeed peculiar.

Suddenly Welsh saw the incredulity on the faces of all three men. Something dangerously resembling a blush fought for recognition on his face as he struggled to regain his composure. 'Hey,' he said, spreading his hands in a helpless gesture. 'I was just a kid when I saw it. It haunted me.' Then his face darkened as he remembered his usual attitude towards Mounties, and the fact that they had returned to haunt him – this time in a less than romantic guise.

Seeking to reassert his authority after the extraordinary response – or lack of one – from the police in Chicago, Bolt was ushering Benton and Thatcher along the train and into the carriage occupied by the horses. Initially unsettled by the nauseating gases emanating from higher up the train, they had been further upset when the Mountie looking after them had slithered unconscious to the floor. Now, with the arrival of Bolt, the horses became distinctly ill-at-ease. None of them, on the musical ride, had been impressed by the director or his crew. They had, in fact, tacitly agreed amongst themselves that there was something 'not quite right' about the nasty, brutish and short man giving orders. The beret was bad enough, but it was the sullen little moustache lurking underneath it that really worried them. If ever a moustache had a few grudges of its own to settle, then this was the one.

Bolt, however, wasn't interested in the horses or their opinion of his facial furniture. Hustling Benton and Thatcher into the carriage at gunpoint and backed up by another member of his gang, he pointed to the comatose Mountie in the corner. 'Howard. Pick him up, will you?'

'Pick him up?' Howard Albee looked doubtfully

at the prone figure. Mounties, he had earlier noticed, were generally taller and broader than criminals. And this one was one of the biggest.

'Prop him up, then,' corrected Bolt. 'Against the door.'

With a sigh of relief, Albee did as he was bid.

'Now then,' said Bolt, turning back to his hostages. 'In an effort to show you that my intentions are serious, I was thinking of a gesture you might appreciate.'

As Benton and Thatcher looked on, he opened the sliding door of the carriage and, just as Frobisher and Benton's father had done with the hapless Frankie Moliere, threw the Mountie out of the train.

'Oh my God!' Horrified, Thatcher watched as the train hurtled past a small farmhouse. If the Mountie hadn't already been unconscious, his landing would have rendered him so: he shot like a bullet through the open front window of the house and, unseen by the occupants of the train, landed on a dining-room table. The farmer and his wife, who had long run out of conversation, looked up as their lunch went flying. Then they experienced the same, fleeting thought. Here was something to talk about. A topic. Then, as they stared at the prone Mountie in front of them, they abandoned that thought. Starting a conversation was just too much effort. And who was to say it would be an interesting conversation anyway? They continued to munch in silence.

Back on the train and grinning from ear to ear, Bolt turned back to Benton and Thatcher. 'You see? We mean business. But,' he added, 'we do have a sense of humour. You,' he said to Benton, 'put your arms round her.'

'I beg your pardon?'

'Put your arms round her. Like you were hugging her.'

'But . . .'

'Just do it!' Albee jabbed his gun into the small of Benton's back.

'Alright . . . um . . .' Hugely embarrassed, Benton placed his arms round Thatcher's waist. 'I'm sorry, sir . . . I don't appear to have any choice in . . .'

'And you,' bellowed Bolt to Thatcher, 'do likewise.'

Without a word, Thatcher obeyed. Her poker face betrayed no emotion whatsoever as she placed her hands around the taut, finely-tuned muscles of Benton's broad back. Not even by a flicker of her eyelids did she show her feelings as her brown eyes met Benton's blue ones. Even when Albee clicked the two pairs of handcuffs behind their backs, locking them into an embrace, she remained impassive.

'Now this really amuses me,' chuckled Bolt. 'Superior officer. Junior officer. Boss,' he said as he prodded Thatcher's side. 'Worker,' he leered at

Benton. 'The empowered. The unempowered. And look, they're even hugging each other. It's a beautiful thing, don't you think?'

'What,' said Benton, fighting to keep his composure, 'do you hope to gain from this?'

'Oh, you couldn't possibly imagine,' laughed Bolt. 'Well . . . maybe you could. Start by thinking: choo, choo, choo – train. Now think,' he said as he slammed a fist into the palm of his other hand, 'kaboom! Explosives. Then put the two together. Train. Boom. Explosives.' Then, laughing at his own extraordinary wit, he headed towards the door. As he reached it, he turned and, remembering he was a terrorist and not a comedian, looked to Albee. 'If they move,' he said, 'shoot them.'

Silence – broken only by the occasional nervous whinny of a horse – descended in the carriage. Benton didn't know where to look. To say that he was uncomfortably close to his superior officer was an understatement: he was positively wrapped round her. Being nearly a head taller than Thatcher, he found that staring at her forehead was his least embarrassing option. Thatcher herself found the situation even more difficult. She found – as Bolt had discovered – that she fitted snugly into Benton's arms and that even if she tilted her head to one side, she was still staring at his shoulders. Her most comfortable position was staring straight ahead – at the adam's apple two inches from her face.

The silence became unbearable after thirty seconds. 'The men,' said Thatcher in as businesslike a voice as she could muster. 'They're not dead, are they, Fraser?' As she said the words, she looked up at him – and immediately regretted the reflex action. Eye contact was all very well, but at a distance. There was something extremely disconcerting about it in such close proximity.

'No, ma'am,' replied Benton in a whisper. The title 'ma'am' came easily to him this time. There was absolutely nothing sir-like about the body pressed against him. 'Er . . . as we passed through the ride car I detected the after-odour of the quixotimon root. It is found exclusively,' he explained, 'in the upper reaches of the Amazon basin. In its gaseous form it's known as quixotimanophyl – a paralytic. It's harmless, but the men won't regain consciousness for approximately twenty-six minutes.'

'Say no more,' replied Thatcher. Then, trying desperately to focus on the situation in general and not her own particular dilemma, she prodded Benton in the back.

Surprised, he looked down at her. 'Um . . .'

Thatcher silenced him with her gimlet eyes and, with an almost imperceptible tilt of her head, indicated Albee, sitting on a box of feed beside them.

The gesture was enough: Thatcher wanted to distract their guard. Benton nodded.

'Excuse me?' said Thatcher, turning as far as she could to the man in the green baseball cap.

'Yeah?' Albee tried, and failed, to sound uninterested. In a previous and even more precarious life he had been an actor and, while that career was no more, the craving for attention was as strong as ever.

Thatcher threw him a dazzling smile. 'What's your name?'

'Albee,' said Albee.

'Albee? The same as the playwright?'

'Yes, ma'am.'

'Oh. Are you related, then?'

'Yes, ma'am,' lied Albee. 'We're a theatrical family, see? He writes and I act. Perhaps,' he added as he peeled off his cap with a flourish, 'you recognize me?'

'Um . . . yes. . . Yes! I think I do. You were in . . .?'

'*High Octane Action at Hell Hole Gulch*.' Albee puffed out his chest with pride. 'That was my most recent film.'

'Yes. Yes, I remember. That was one of Robert's favourites.'

'Robert?'

'De Niro.'

'Robert de Niro!' Albee shot up from the feed box and stared in admiration at Thatcher. 'He's my hero. I based my whole character on him. And,' he asked in awe as he stepped closer, 'you *know* him?' Such a small world, he thought as he beamed at the handcuffed woman. Who would have thought the spheres of acting and terrorism would collide so fortuitously?

'Dated him,' replied Thatcher.

'You . . . *dated* . . . Robert de Niro?'

'Yep. He gave me a tattoo.' Thatcher gestured as best she could. 'On my hip.'

This Albee had to see. He knew his hero was something of an artist in his spare time – and here was the chance to see an original work by the great man! Too excited even to ask permission for a viewing, he bent down beside Thatcher.

She reacted like lightning. With a small grunt of triumph, she swung her leg and walloped Albee in the temple. Stunned by the blow, her victim fell forward towards Benton, who, in turn, kneed him in exactly the same place. Albee let out a feeble moan and tumbled unconscious to the floor.

'Very nice work, ma'am,' grinned Benton.

'Er . . . thank you Fraser.' Embarrassed by the thought that Benton might misread the fact that her heart was hammering in her chest, Thatcher looked away. The silence that followed was even more loaded with tension than the previous one. The fact that there was no longer anyone watching over them made the situation far more embarrassing. Both had been in similar clinches before: neither knew how to handle the unnatural circumstances of this one.

This time it was Benton who spoke first. As he did so, Thatcher looked up at him and was more than a little disconcerted by the way he seemed to be examining her face and hair. His gaze swept over her, not flinching and not missing an inch.

'May I?' he enquired as they locked eyes.

'May you what?' snapped Thatcher.

Instead of replying, Benton leaned forward. Thatcher gasped as she felt his breath against her cheek; her eyes widened as his mouth opened, revealing his perfect white teeth and pink tongue. Rigid with what she tried to persuade herself was horror, she waited for his mouth to descend on hers.

It didn't. It bypassed her face and stopped just beyond her left ear. 'Er. . . Fraser? What are you doing?' And then a sharp tug and a movement in her hair told her exactly what he was doing – removing one of her hairpins. When he emerged from behind the ear he was holding it between his teeth.

Startled, confused (but not, she told herself, disappointed), Thatcher stared at him as he chewed at the small object. It was only when he leaned towards her again that she realized he hadn't been chewing: he had manoeuvred the pin so that he was now holding one prong between his teeth. And now he was inviting her to clench at the other prong in order to straighten the pin.

Nodding her understanding, ignoring her disappointment, Thatcher parted her lips, revealing her own very white and very expensive teeth. And then disappointment gave way to something altogether more confusing as her mouth met Benton's. Their lips played together as she tried to grasp the proffered prong. In theory, she thought, this should be easy. In practice, however, their tongues kept getting in the way as Benton guided the small object between her teeth. But at last she had it and, tugging away from Benton, she felt it straighten and lengthen . . .

And then, as she released her end, Benton dropped the pin. It fell on to the open neck of her tunic, hovered tentatively on the lapel – and then fell into her cleavage.

Their eyes met again. Disappointment met with daring: both knew what had to be done, and both pretended they didn't want to do it. Giving Benton tacit approval, Thatcher nodded and, to illustrate that this was business and *not* pleasure, took a deep, resigned breath. The action proved unwise: the hairpin, spotting more cleavage, burrowed downwards.

Benton pretended not to notice. Heaving his own sigh, he angled his head into her blouse and began to fish around with his teeth. Not entirely sure what to do under such unusual circumstances, and conscious that Benton's stance forced her head even more tightly against his chest, she adopted a glazed, totally blank expression.

A few seconds later Benton's tongue flicked against her naked flesh and his head stopped moving. A moment after that he emerged, eyes shining, the pin once again between his teeth. Then he lunged forward over her shoulder and dropped the pin into his hands. With his nimble fingers working at the handcuff, he began to pick at the locking mechanism. In order to see what he was doing, however, he was obliged to rest his head on Thatcher's shoulder. Desperate to break the renewed, strained silence, he said the first thing that came into his head. 'Escada?'

'I beg your pardon?'

'That fragrance you're wearing.'

'No.'

'Cartier?'

'No.'

'Oh.' Then, suddenly, the lock snapped open and Benton was free. 'Chanel?' he asked as his hands slipped free of their bonds.

'Plee . . . ease,' said Thatcher, to whom Chanel was beneath contempt.

'I give up,' smiled Benton as he leaned away from her. 'What is the perfume you're wearing?'

Benton's hands were free – but Thatcher's were still manacled in a vice-like grip around his back. The situation made her feel both powerful and vulnerable – her favourite feeling. As ever, it was the powerful part that took over. 'I'm not wearing anything, Fraser,' she snapped as she stared into his eyes. 'I hate perfume.'

In Chicago, Ray was preparing for his role as a conduit. As he didn't know precisely what a conduit was, his preparation was minimal. Nor did it require much thought: he would find life easier, Welsh had told him, if he left the thinking to Agent Ford and simply did as he was told. 'If you obey orders,' Welsh had finished, 'then you won't be held responsible when things go wrong, will you?'

Ford's orders were simple. Ray was to take a bag containing ten million dollars, by helicopter, to station siding thirty-three on the Palliser Line. There the station manager would show him how to attach the bag to the mail pole – and then he would leave.

'Supposing,' said Ray with one last, admittedly feeble attempt at mutiny, 'it's all a hoax?'

'It's not a hoax,' barked Ford. 'We've just had confirmation of the hijacking from a Mountie they threw off the train.'

'They threw a Mountie off the train? Is he alright?'

'Seems so,' shrugged Ford. 'A pecan pie broke his fall.'

'A *what?*'

'A pecan pie. What are you – Canadian or something?'

'No. I'm American. Italian-American, if you must know, but what's that got to do with . . .'

'. . . Just go, will ya'!' screamed Ford. 'And, oh, Detective . . . one last thing.'

'Yes?'

'The dog stays here.'

Ray looked down at the expectant Diefenbaker. 'Sorry, Dief,' he said, 'but orders is orders.' Then, grinning, he looked back at the FBI agent. 'Actually . . . sir, he's not a dog. He's a wolf.'

Ford turned a deathly shade of pale and looked at the creature at Ray's feet. Diefenbaker, taking Ray's cue, began to growl. The sound started at the back of his throat; no more than a low rumbling. Then it increased in volume, reaching terrifying proportions as Dief opened his mouth, displaying a set of lethal, pointed fangs.

Ford opened his own mouth. 'Er . . . Detective?'

'Yes?'

'Perhaps . . . perhaps you should take him after all. Extra manpower. Or,' he added with a strained sickly grin, 'wolfpower.'

Diefenbaker, sporting a happier grin, stepped forward to lick Ford's hand in gratitude.

Strangely, Ford had already left the room.

Ray reached the tiny station siding half an hour later. Nothing more than a wooden shack by the railway line in the middle of a prairie, it looked completely deserted – and incongruous beside the gleaming helicopter that had deposited Ray.

There was no reply to Ray's tentative knock, so, feeling intensely vulnerable, he opened the door and walked into the shack. Any thoughts of being ambushed and annihilated quickly disappeared when he noticed the only occupant of the room. The man sitting dozing in a chair was ancient, wizened and looked, Ray thought, not unlike a prune. A friendly prune, he corrected, as he took in the man's benign expression.

'How you doing?' began Ray with an equally benign smile. 'I'm with the police.'

'You are?' The old man looked impressed – then puzzled. 'Where are they?'

'I'm it.' Ray pointed to his chest. 'I'm the police.'

'You are?' The old man nodded to himself. 'And how do you like it, son? Does it pay well?'

'Yeah,' said Ray, swinging the bag containing more dollars than he would ever earn in his lifetime. 'It's fine. Say – do you have something called a "mail pole"?'

'A what?'

'A "mail pole".'

'Sure.' The ancient nodded to the structure between the shack and the railway line. 'That's it over there. You wanna post some mail?'

'Uh . . . something like that, yeah. What do I do . . . just hang the bag on that clip thing?'

'Yep. But ... uh, you'd better take my socks down first.'

Ray turned round in amazement.

'S'alright,' smiled his companion. 'They'll be dry now.'

Remembering Welsh's entreaties to obey orders at all costs, Ray climbed the steps to the mail pole, removed the socks and attached the bag. As he did so, he heard a rumble in the distance. A moment of sadness engulfed him as he looked down the track. The train, he thought: the hijacked train with my best friend on board.

Some of the occupants of the train, however, were anything but sad. In the caboose, Bolt, Freya Chichester-Clark and the most literary-minded of the gang, Bert Brecht, whooped with delight when they saw the bag of swag dangling on the mail pole. And it was Brecht, as the train hurtled towards it, who extended the snatch pole and lifted the bag on to the train. He missed the half-forlorn, half-angry expression of the man standing at the foot of the steps in front of the station.

As the train sped on towards Chicago, Freya – a whizz at arithmetic – began to count the money while the others went back to their earlier task; that of dismantling their camera equipment and assembling the components of a bomb from various parts of it. 'Clever, eh?' as Bolt had said when he had hatched the plan. The rest of the gang were far too self-obsessed to agree with him. They were, to a man – and Freya – of the opinion that no idea was good unless it was theirs.

As they finished constructing the bomb, Bolt had another idea – one that the others were grudgingly obliged to agree with. 'That old geyser who went to the bathroom,' he said. 'He's still around somewhere. Go find him, Bert, and give him the old heave-ho, okay?'

Bert nodded his assent, relishing the idea of yet another Mountie flying out of the train.

Frobisher was unaware of his impending fate. Back in the bathroom – for reasons not unrelated to moose and gorgonzola – he was delighted to see Benton and Thatcher lurking outside when he had finished his ablutions. 'Ah,' he said, doffing his hat at the latter. 'Allow me to debrief you. I have just assessed the situation in the engine room of this vehicle . . .'

'. . . and?'

'And . . . ma'am . . . the enemy has bypassed the brake valves. In a nutshell? This train is a runaway.'

'Not only is it a runaway, sir,' said Benton, 'I think it's loaded with explosives.' Benton had finally worked out what had disturbed him about the camera equipment: a detonator, no matter how much you tried to disguise it as a microphone, was still a detonator.

Not to be outdone in the revelation department, Frobisher gestured behind him. 'The station back there? They took something off a mail pole.'

Thatcher nodded. 'Ransom.'

'Which leaves,' said Benton, 'only one conclusion. The ransom was a cover. Their darker purpose is to drive this bomb into the heart of Chicago . . .'

As he spoke, all three of them heard footsteps approaching: not from behind or in front of them – they had locked the doors on either side – but from above. Someone was on the roof of the train.

Thatcher whirled round to Frobisher. 'Do you have a gun?'

'No. I left it at the border.'

'Likewise,' said Benton.

'Damn.'

'It's the law, ma'am,' said Benton. 'We're not allowed to use guns in the United States.'

'I'm well aware of that Fraser,' snapped Thatcher. Still smarting over the cleavage-nuzzling episode, she was relishing re-asserting her authority. 'If we survive this,' she added, 'remind me to make some changes to my official travel policy.'

'Yes, ma'am. In the meantime, I think I'd better get out on the roof and assess the situation.'

Concern creased Thatcher's features. Just because she was smarting over what had happened in the horse carriage didn't mean that she was totally opposed to it happening again. 'I'm not sure if that's altogether wise, Fraser.'

But Benton had already decided that, wise or not, it was a necessary course of action to take. 'Stand clear!' he commanded as he unlocked the door of the utility carriage and, just in case one of the hijackers was standing on the other side, kicked it open. On the other side, Bert Brecht went flying.

'Ha!' said Benton in satisfaction as he leaped over the prone figure of the stunned terrorist. Without so much as a pause for breath, he ran down the length of the carriage, wrenched open the other door and, flinching slightly at the sudden chill of the wind, braced himself to climb the ladder on the outside platform. Any hesitation or second thoughts were banished as he looked over his shoulder to see Brecht, his face a mask of anger, running towards him. He was carrying an axe.

At the other end of the carriage, Frobisher and Thatcher looked on. 'Well,' said the former, stepping forward, 'he's going to need some help.'

'No!' In a theatrical gesture, possibly and unconsciously gleaned from her hijackers, Thatcher stopped him with an authoritative hand. 'I'm the senior officer. It's my responsibility.' Without giving Frobisher a chance to protest (which, in the light of his rheumatism and the unhappy combination of moose and gorgonzola, he had no intention of doing), she ran down the corridor.

By the time she had scaled the ladder, Benton and Brecht were locked in hand to hand combat on the roof of the train. Thatcher stood, gripping the top rung of the ladder, assessing the situation. Brecht's feet were only inches from her hands – and were coming closer. Smiling with grim satisfaction, she reached forward, ready to deliver a stinging and crippling blow to his ankles.

Then Benton saw her. 'Uh . . . ma'am. I really would prefer that you not . . .'

But it was too late. Thatcher delivered an impressive karate chop to the back of Brecht's legs. Stunned by the blow, he lost his footing and toppled backwards. For a moment he seemed to hang suspended in mid-air. Then, with a wail of terror, he fell off the roof of the train and into the lethal depths of the canyon below.

It was only then that Thatcher realized her mistake. Brecht's hands, as she delivered the blow, had been holding Benton's lapels in a vice-like grip – and they were still clinging tightly as he tumbled into the abyss. Thatcher caught a glimpse of Benton's mouth, wide open with shock, as he disappeared with the hijacker.

The train thundered on, oblivious to the fact that it had lost two more of its occupants.

Chapter Four

'It was all my fault!'

Buck Frobisher looked uneasily across the little room. Being locked in the tiny toilet of a runaway train with a wailing woman was an experience he had no wish to repeat. He had never, anyway, been very good at consoling people. His usual method of dealing with stress – even bereavement – was to tell people to pull themselves together and do something positive. When he had lost Caroline to Bob Fraser he had, for example, grabbed a shotgun and trundled off to shoot a few elk. That had cheered him up no end.

But elk-shooting, in this particular case, really didn't seem a viable option. Aware that Thatcher was waiting for him to say something, he cleared his throat and told her that, no, it wasn't her fault.

The remark was greeted with a derisive snort – but not from Thatcher. Turning to his left, Frobisher saw that Bob Fraser was standing right beside him. 'Well,' he said when he had finished snorting, 'in a way it *was* her fault, you know.'

'Stay out of this,' snapped Frobisher.

'How can I stay out of it?' wailed Thatcher. 'I am

the senior officer on board this train. Fraser was my immediate staff. He was,' she added as she sniffed into a tissue, 'my responsibility.'

'She has a point, Buck,' said Bob, who seemed remarkably sanguine about losing his only son to an abyss.

'He drove me crazy,' sniffed Thatcher. 'That's no secret. But . . . but lately I had started to think . . . I mean . . . I had started to feel . . . .'

'Oh great Scott,' sighed Bob as realization dawned. 'You don't think she . . . ?'

'Great Scott,' said Frobisher to the distressed woman. 'You don't suppose that you're . . .'

Thatcher looked, pain and puzzlement in her eyes, at the elderly man. 'I'm confused, sergeant. My feelings are very confused.'

Frobisher went bright red. Feelings were his least favourite thing. If you had to have them, he reckoned, at least you should have the decency to keep them to yourself. This woman seemed to have fallen victim to that horrible American trend of sharing them. 'I see,' he said by way of consolation.

'*I see?*' squeaked Bob. 'What kind of counsel is that? Console her, for God's sake!'

Aware that if he responded to his dead friend, Thatcher would think he was talking to her, Frobisher refrained from delivering the unpleasant rebuke that lay on the tip of his tongue. Instead, and even more embarrassed now, he cleared his throat again and addressed the disconsolate Mountie. 'Uh, Inspector ... there are times between women and men ... that is to say, there are times between men and women when things grow ... arise ...' Steeling himself to utter the dreaded word, he looked Thatcher in the eye. 'Feelings.' He delivered the word with a sort of spitting motion and a curl of the lip – as if divesting himself of something even more unpleasant than the unfortunate moose and gorgonzola. 'Well,' he added, glad that the counselling session was over. 'Enough said.'

'*Enough said?*'

Frobisher stoically ignored the presence at his side, while making a mental note to tackle Bob at a later stage on the subject of feelings. When alive, Bob's attitude to them had been much the same as his own. Death, it was becoming ever more apparent, did strange things to people.

Yet to Frobisher's surprise, his words of wisdom seemed to have had a calming effect on Thatcher. 'You're right, Sergeant,' she said in a suddenly business-like voice. 'We've got a train to stop. We have to push on.' Then she stood up, adjusted her uniform, ran a hand through her hair and reached for the door handle. 'You deal with the men. I'll take the engine.' With one purposeful stride, she exited the bathroom.

Bob Fraser looked on in admiration as she closed

the door behind her. 'She really takes death in her stride, doesn't she?'

Frobisher nodded. 'But you don't think Benton's really dead, do you?'

'No. My guess is he's executing a plan to bring this crisis to an end.'

He was. Never one to panic in a crisis, Benton had, in one split second as he fell from the train, weighed up his options. One was to follow Brecht to the bottom of the canyon and to die. The other, as Brecht's hands released their hold, was to lunge for the minute ledge between the railway tracks and oblivion. This he did – and with gratifying success. He lay there, panting with exertion and relief as the train rattled past him. Then, rising to his feet and brushing himself down, he considered his next set of options. In that he was aided by the rickety handcar standing on the spur of track that led off the main line. He wasted not a second. Jumping on, he wrenched at the see-saw hand mechanism. After a few protesting squeaks and squeals, the rusty iron wheels of the car began to move. Then, establishing a regular pumping rhythm, he directed the little vehicle on to the main track and in pursuit of the train. It wasn't, he thought, the fastest mode of transport on earth, but it would have to suffice. And as he pumped up and down, he was pleased to discover that the little car gathered its own momentum, going ever faster – and ever nearer the train.

By the time Thatcher had made her resolution to pull herself together and reserve her grief for a later, private and intense moment, Benton was swinging a lasso above his head, aiming its loop at the buffers on the back of the train. And by the time she had made her way – clinging to the outside of the train – to the next carriage, Benton had thrown the lasso, attached it to the train, and was pulling himself and his car towards the train. And so when Thatcher decided her best route to the engine was along the roof, she had no idea that Benton was back on board. Her surprise, then, was total when Benton appeared, seemingly from nowhere, at the foot of the ladder she was about to climb.

'Fraser!'

'Ma'am.' Fraser doffed his hat (an old hand at surviving near-death experiences) and looked at her in concern. 'Thank God you're alright.'

In a passable imitation of a dead fish, Thatcher gawped at her deputy. Then she blinked several times and, frightened that her knees were about to give way, clutched at the ladder for support. Aware, finally, that she resembled a deceased cod, she cleared her throat. 'I thought,' she whispered, 'that you were . . .'

'. . . Dead? No ma'am.'

'But how did you . . .?'

Benton brushed the question aside with an

impatient wave of his hand. 'That's not important. What is important is that . . .'

'Not important?' Relief and surprise had, as was often the way with Thatcher, given way to anger. '*Not important?* I *grieved* for you.'

'You did?' Benton was childishly delighted.

'Briefly,' snapped Thatcher.

'Understood.' Yet in the moment that was far briefer than Thatcher's grief, a strange sensation tingled down Benton's spine. 'Red suits you,' he said, unnerved by the tingle. Thatcher tried and failed to summon a disapproving look. She, too, was tingling. Briefly.

'Now,' said Benton, after the moment had passed. 'I've had some time to think about it, and it's my conclusion that, given the nature of our situation, and the threat that we pose, the only logical course of action for the authorities will be to destroy this train.'

Thatcher was horrified. 'And everyone on board?'

'Yes, ma'am.'

'That's madness.'

'Well . . . put yourself in their situation,' said Benton with a shrug. 'Wouldn't you do the same?'

Again, Thatcher was appalled – but for different reasons. 'You think I could be that cold-hearted?'

Benton had the grace to look slightly sheepish, yet stuck to his guns. 'Well, forgive me ma'am, but

I would have thought you more than up to the challenge.'

Thatcher looked as if her world had fallen apart. 'Is that,' she whispered, 'what you think of me?'

'I don't mean to upset you . . .'

'I'm not upset, Fraser!' The whisper had fled, chased away by an angry bark.

Looking uncomfortable, Benton tried to explain. 'It's just that. . . well, what I'm trying to explain is . . .'

But Thatcher didn't want explanations. 'Don't bother,' she snapped as she reached again for the ladder. 'Let's go.'

Shrugging, Benton stood patiently as she clambered on to the roof of the train. Then, careful not to follow her too closely in case he made contact with the area sporting Robert De Niro's tattoo, he reached for the rungs and began to climb.

By the time he reached the roof, Thatcher was stalking towards the front of the train. Everything about her body language suggested that she was, after all, deeply upset. And if Benton needed any confirmation of that fact, he was given it when she stopped, mid-stomp, and turned as he hurried towards her. 'Actually, Fraser, I *am* upset. What makes you think,' she asked as he skidded to a halt in front of her, 'that we're so different? You graduated first in your class and so did I. You received medals for field work, as did I.' Almost as close as she had been when they had been handcuffed together, she tapped his chest. 'You wear red serge: I wear red serge. The only difference between us is that you are a woman and I'm not.'

'Er ... I think you have that back to front, ma'am.'

Thatcher looked straight into his eyes. 'You know what I mean.'

'Yes,' said Benton. 'I do.'

'I'm not made of stone.'

'I'm very much aware of that.'

'Are you?' Somehow they had moved closer: so close that Thatcher was sure Benton could hear her heart racing.

'Yes,' said Benton.

'You are?'

'Yes.' Benton leaned even closer. 'I know you have a heart. And I think it beats in just the same way as mine.'

If it keeps missing a beat, thought Thatcher, then, yes, it's just the same. 'What,' she breathed. 'is it doing right now?'

'It's racing.'

'Out of control?'

Benton nodded. 'It's a runaway.' As he spoke, he knew there was no way of controlling the situation. And from the look in Thatcher's eyes; the way she inclined her head slightly to one side and parted her lips, he knew that she knew there was nothing they could do. Except, of course, kiss.

The next thing Thatcher was aware of was sinking into Benton's arms, of being kissed and returning those kisses with equal passion. Like him, she was oblivious to everything except The Moment. And, as Moments went, it was fairly lengthy.

It was broken, not by the tunnel into which the train shrieked; not by the fact that the tunnel roof shaved off the top of Benton's hat; and not through any desire to stop what they were doing – but by Frobisher's head popping urgently from a hatch in the roof of the carriage not five feet from where they were standing.

'Uh,' said the elderly man as he took in the situation. 'Hum. I'm not one to throw water on a decent fire, but something is amiss. The enemy,' he added by way of explanation, 'is gathering in the caboose.'

His words had a dramatic effect. Benton and Thatcher pulled away from each other as if they had been electrocuted; both smoothed down their uniforms; both tried to pretend they weren't actually there and then, when that failed, they both answered Frobisher at the same time. 'We were just,' they said in unison, 'just . . . um . . .'

'Strategy session,' interrupted Frobisher. 'I understand.' Then, hoping he had niftily avoided the need to discuss Feelings, he popped back down into the train.

Above him, Thatcher and Benton looked at each other. Then, without a word, Thatcher assumed a haughty, Thatcherite expression and stalked off towards the hatch in the roof. Benton stood still for a moment, a strange, slightly wistful expression on his face. Then, straightening his shoulders, shrugging away the past few minutes, he followed her below.

Ray had forgotten his earlier moment of sadness. Benton, he knew, would be doing his utmost to save the day, the train and its precious cargo. Benny, he thought, might be intensely irritating at times – but he was resourceful all the time. There was no need to dwell on the danger in the train.

Besides, there were much better things on which to dwell. Foremost amongst them was the fact that he no longer had the supercilious Ford breathing over his shoulder; had no more dreaded orders to obey. Ford's instructions had ended with the delivery of the money.

I'll show him, thought Ray as, after the train had disappeared into the distance, he trudged back into the station shack. A plan was already forming in his mind. To execute it, he would need the assistance of the ancient station manager.

Ray smiled broadly – an unnerving sight – as he closed the door behind him. 'Got your socks,' he said, handing them over.

'Well done, well done. And bone dry, I see. Nothing like a mail pole.' The old man nodded in satisfaction and deposited the footwear on his desk. At least Ray assumed it was a desk: it was difficult to see what might lurk under the unholy mess in front of him.

'Say,' continued Ray, 'what's your name?'

'Crew,' said the old man.

'Crew. Ha ha. That's kinda neat.'

'Is it?'

'Yeah . . . you know. Train . . . Crew. It's good. I like it.'

Not entirely sure what his visitor's point was, Thomas Crew smiled uneasily. 'Er . . . what's yours, son?'

'My what?'

'Your name.'

'Oh. Vecchio. Ray Vecchio.'

'Hmm,' Crew looked distinctly unimpressed. 'Sounds foreign to me.'

Ray correctly deduced that this line of conversation was not worth pursuing. Crew was probably one of those Mid-Westerners who regarded anyone from the next state as foreign and, as such, not to be trusted. Better stick to trains, he thought. He looked, not entirely hopefully, at the appalling heap of junk on the desk. 'I was thinking,' he began. 'Have you got any way to track trains? Some kind of grid or a computer or something?'

To Ray's surprise, Crew nodded and sprang to his feet. 'Sure, they gave me a computer, but it's a useless piece of junk. Technology – pah!' he spat as he lifted an old coat off the desk to reveal a new and highly expensive computer. 'There's nothing on this but fish. Look,' he finished as he pointed to the screen. 'Little fish swimming around.'

Ray suppressed a giggle. 'Er . . . they call that a screen saver.'

Then he bounded forward, tapped on the keyboard and, to Crew's amazement, turned the fish into a railway grid.

'Hey!' said a deeply impressed Crew. 'You some kind of expert?'

'Uh . . . well, kind of, I suppose. They teach us this kind of thing in police school.'

Crew's admiration gave way to derision. 'Huh. No wonder you guys never solve crimes any more. Too busy playing with toys.'

'Well,' said Ray. 'They do have their uses. See here . . . this is a pattern of the Palliser Line and that,' he added as he pointed to a line snaking across the screen, 'is our runaway train.'

'Say! Whaddya' know!' Delighted with the new toy, Crew pulled up a chair and looked on as Ray monitored the progress of the train. After a few minutes, he peered more closely at the screen. 'Seems like they've slowed down.'

'Mmm.' Ray stroked his chin. 'Wonder why.'

The next minute, and to his utter horror, the train vanished completely off the screen. 'Hey!' he yelled. 'Where the hell have they gone?'

Beside him, Crew was looking smug. 'Told you it was a useless piece of junk.'

Fuming, Ray jabbed furiously at the keyboard in front of him – but to no avail. The runaway train resolutely refused to return to the screen.

'That lump,' said Crew, peering at the screen. 'Would it indicate a hill?'

'Could do,' shrugged Ray, whose interest in hills was, at this juncture, non-existent.

'Well,' continued the other man, 'if so, it's Horseback Ridge.'

Ray turned round. 'Am I missing something here? What has a hill called Horseback Ridge got to do with our train?'

'Quite a lot,' replied Crew, ignoring the sarcasm. 'There's an old shunt line by the hill. Train's gone off the screen ... reckon that's where it's gone.' Nodding to himself, Crew opened the drawer beneath him and pulled out an ancient scroll map. 'Here,' he said as he unfolded it. 'I'll show you. This line,' he pointed, 'is the Palliser Line. That there is Horseback Ridge ... and *this* – this is where your runaway's gone.'

Ray looked at where the gnarled old finger was pointing. 'So where does the shunt line lead to?'

'A nuclear plant. But,' said Crew, stalling Ray

mid-wail, 'your train won't make it there – 'cos at this time of day there's another train coming this way, carrying spent fuel rods.'

'Why the hell,' said Ray with a frown, 'would they want to divert . . . oh my God! Fuel rods?'

'Yep. It's a train full of radioactive uranium.'

'So if that train meets up with our train, and if our train's wired . . .' Horrified at the vision that sprang in his head, Ray jumped to his feet. 'You got a car?'

Crew broke into a broad, enthusiastic grin that seemed to knock decades off him. 'Have I got a car?' he chuckled. 'Oh boy do I have a car!'

Relieved, although slightly puzzled, Ray ran towards the door. 'Then let's go!'

A minute later, the reason for Crew's boyish enthusiasm was revealed. Leading Ray to a lean-to beside the station, he tugged at a length of tarpaulin, exposing one of the newest and nippiest vehicles on the market. Related – via satellite by the look of it – to the jeep family, it had chunky exposed wheels, a serious-looking roll bar, no roof and a gleaming, half-exposed chrome engine.

'This,' said an astonished Ray, 'is yours?'

'Yep.' Beaming with pride, Crew surveyed his baby. Then he leaned into the space behind the seats and emerged with two crash helmets. 'Here,' he said as he handed one to Ray. 'Better put this on. It's going to be a bumpy ride.'

'You don't happen to have a third helmet, do you?' asked Ray.

'No. There's no room for a third person. Anyway,' added Crew, looking around. 'Who else is there to take with us?'

'I .. er, I wasn't thinking about a person. It's just that I tied my . . . my dog up outside and figured he might like the ride. Thought he might be getting . . . you know, lonely.'

'Sure.' Belying his age, Crew hurdled nimbly over the driver's door of the vehicle. 'But he's not a lap dog, is he? Don't want him falling out.'

'Um, no. Not a lap dog. Definitely not.' Ray walked back to the shack where Diefenbaker, for want of anything better to do, had fallen asleep. He was in for a very rude and violent awakening.

Five minutes later Diefenbaker was beginning to wish Crew had not extended the kind invitation to join them in the jeep. Despite the lack of anything remotely resembling a road – or even a flat surface – Crew screamed along at more miles an hour than Diefenbaker knew existed. Even Ray, a great fan of driving at speed, looked slightly sick. And heaven only knew, thought Dief as he cowered at Ray's feet, how Ray could possibly read a map under these conditions.

'What's this?' shouted Ray above the din of the engine.

'What's what?'

'This.' Ray jabbed a finger at a line on the map.

Crew, whose eyesight was failing, had to take his eyes off the lack of road. This didn't seem to bother him unduly: the vehicle was capable of tackling any terrain – and no animate object would be stupid enough to stray into its erratic path. 'That,' he shouted as he looked at where Ray was pointing on the railway, 'is a safety measure. An emergency run-off shunt.'

'Do you think we can get our train onto it?'

'Sure. If we put on a bit of speed.'

Oh God, thought Diefenbaker, eavesdropping. That's all I need.

'And do you think,' yelled Ray as Crew stepped even harder on the throttle, 'you can get me on the train?'

Crew had to mull over that one for a moment. 'Well, it'll pass under a bridge in about ten minutes. Depends if you fancy jumping off the bridge on to the roof.'

Ray didn't fancy that very much at all. There was, however, no alternative. The best thing to do, as Crew went on to explain, was for Ray to get to the train while Crew drove on to the shunt and switched the rails.

Ray agreed. Getting to the train was imperative. He needed to alert Benton to the fact that the hijackers were not the only threat: to tell him that Ford and his cronies were intending to blow the train up as a damage limitation exercise.

In Chicago, however, Ford's plans were beginning to fall apart. Like Crew, he had a state of the art computer that monitored the train – and subsequently lost it. But unlike Crew, he didn't have a twenty-year old, coffee-stained map to fall back on.
'We've lost them!' he screamed into the computer. 'The train's disappeared!'
'Oh.'
'What do you mean "oh"?' Ford swung round to Deeter. 'Is that all you can say?'
'No, sir. I agree that losing them is bad news – but we also have some good news.'
'And what's that? They've been whisked away by aliens?'
'No, sir.' Deeter held up a fax that had come through moments before. 'We've matched the voice on the tape.'
'Oh. Who is he?'
'Bolt,' read Deeter. 'Randall K. Sometimes calls himself Robert. Born Oregon, 1953. Ex-military. And,' he added with a curl of his lip, 'he's a demolitions expert.'
'Shit!'
'Dishonourably discharged,' continued Deeter, 'in 1987 following an explosion at an officer's mess in Baden-Baden. Went underground stateside and resurfaced in a white supremacist group called the

Fathers of the Confederation, based in Idaho.' Deeter grimaced and looked up at Ford. 'He's been linked to a number of recent bombings and train derailments.'

'So how did he find time to become a film director?'

Deeter looked down at the fax again. 'I'm afraid we don't have any information on that, sir. Perhaps he isn't really a film director. Maybe that was just a cover.'

'For what?'

'For being a terrorist.'

'Oh. Yes, I see. Well, Deeter, as soon as we . . . hey!' Swinging back to the screen again, Ford noticed a succession of dots bleeping in the corner. 'We've got the train back!'

'Well done, sir.'

'Thank you.' Ford bent towards the machine. 'Right. As soon as we can establish a failsafe position, we get the Rapid Response Team in and hit the train with everything we've got.'

'We're going to blow up the train?'

Ford shot his deputy a withering, old-fashioned look. 'You'd rather blow up Chicago?'

Chapter Five

Tactfully ignoring Thatcher and Benton's rumpled appearance and sheepish expressions, Frobisher helped them through the hatch in the train's roof and led them through the vehicle, past the still-comatose Mounties and to the partition at the caboose. 'The enemy,' he said as they all huddled into the alcove, 'has gathered in the caboose.'

Cutting an authoritative figure despite the shaved crown of his hat, Benton held up a commanding hand. 'Alright. Follow me.'

'No.' Thatcher's voice was like a whip-crack.

'Ma'am?'

'This is my detail, Fraser. I'll go first. You follow me.'

Without leaving time for further objections, Thatcher stepped forward, pushed her way through the door and on to the outside platform.

Both taken aback by her sudden reversion to imperiousness, Benton and Frobisher looked at each other, a tacit sigh of 'women' on their lips. Someone else, however, had a typically vociferous response. 'Boy,' sighed Bob Fraser, materializing in front of them, 'times change! On balance I think for the better – but in my day a woman wouldn't have been allowed . . .'

'Do you mind?' said Benton and Frobisher in unison. Then, realization dawning, they looked, open-mouthed, at each other. 'Great Scott!' Again they spoke simultaneously. 'You mean that you can actually see . . .'

'Fellows,' interrupted Benton's father. 'This is not a good time to ponder one of death's mysteries.' Then he shot a half-puzzled, half-accusing look at his son. 'What happened to your hat?'

'Nothing.' Benton would sooner have had half of his head lopped off than tell his father about what had happened between him and Thatcher.

Bob Fraser nodded. 'Understood.'

'Ready?' said Benton to Frobisher. Then, at the older man's nod, he pushed the door open and followed Thatcher on to the platform. He stopped, mid-stride, when he took in the sight before him. Thatcher was standing on the corresponding platform of the caboose. Bolt was standing beside her. So, holding a gun to Thatcher's head, was a grinning Freya Chichester-Clark.

Bolt beamed at the Mounties. 'Well, howdy gentlemen.' Then, indicating the terrified Thatcher, he shrugged in apology. 'Look, first of all, I want you to know that I have no quarrel with you personally. As a matter of fact, I really love the horsey thing you do. Actually, it kinda turns me on. But,' he added with another shrug, 'the American Government is an outlaw government, because it is a government that has chosen to betray the sacred trust of its founding fathers. That betrayal cannot be tolerated and that so-called government must be punished, you see. So,' he said, holding up a tiny transmitter in his left hand, 'I have decided to take this opportunity to demonstrate a little trick I've been working on with this radio frequency transmitter.' Grinning from ear to ear, he flipped a switch on the mechanism, activating a little digital counter. 'This train is bound for glory,' he announced. 'It is now a trigger mechanism for an imminent nuclear meltdown.'

The two Mounties (three to those with ghost-friendly antennae) gaped in horror at the smiling terrorist. That horror increased when Bolt leaned down towards the buffers of the caboose and pulled a lever, detaching the caboose from the rest of the train.

Benton was the first to react. Thatcher's pleading eyes, her quiet desperation impelled him to breach the increasing space between their platform and the caboose – but Frobisher held him back. 'No, son,' he commanded with surprising authority. 'Priorities.'

Benton didn't take his eyes off Thatcher. 'But, sir . . .'

'Priorities.' Frobisher was adamant.

Still Benton stared at Thatcher. He thought he detected a new, sadly reproachful look in her eyes, yet he couldn't be sure. The caboose, gently rolling backwards, was already too far away for them to see its occupants clearly, while the main part of the train sped onwards towards destruction.

'Buck,' whispered Bob Fraser to his friend. 'Would you have a word with him?'

'About what?'

Lip curling with disapproval, Bob gestured to the distant caboose. 'Her.'

Oh God, thought Frobisher. Feelings. 'Why me?' he wailed. 'He's your son.'

'Well, yeah,' shrugged Bob, 'I know. But I'm dead and my advice has been growing stale recently. Come on,' he urged as he prodded the other man in the ribs and nodded towards Benton. 'Go ahead.'

Glad that Benton was still looking wistfully at the retreating caboose, Frobisher moved behind him and addressed his left collar-bone. 'Er . . . Benton . . .' Pausing to clear his throat, he decided to start again. 'Benton. Your mother . . . your mother married a good man.'

'Yes,' said Benton, without much conviction and still without turning round. 'She did.'

'I suppose, in a way, your father and I were rivals. But in the end we forged ahead. We overcame,' he said, nodding to himself, 'no matter what. What I'm ... well, what I mean ... I mean that between men and women there are ... things. There are times between men and women ... things which arise.' Then Frobisher took a deep breath and steeled himself to utter the dreaded word. 'Feelings.'

'She's my superior officer, sir. That's all.'

Frobisher nearly fainted with relief. 'Well,' he said with a smile. 'Enough said.'

Bob, who had made a tactful retreat while Frobisher dispensed his advice, noticed that the difficult, intimate conversation appeared to be over. 'All done?' he whispered as he sidled up to Frobisher.

Frobisher turned round and smiled. 'Yep.'

Beside them, Benton also turned. The pained, wistful look had gone. In its place was a resolute, unsmiling determination. 'Right,' he said. 'Let's get back to business.'

At that very moment the train passed under a bridge. Unseen by the three men on the platform, Ray Vecchio was standing on the bridge. Diefenbaker, looking acutely embarrassed and not a little silly, was in his arms. I am a wolf, he kept repeating to himself. Not a lap dog.

Ray screwed his eyes tightly shut and, heart thumping in his breast, braced himself for the jump. 'One ... two ... three ... Go!' Behind him and standing beside the jeep, Crew shouted the command as the train whistled underneath. Leaving no room for misunderstanding, he gave Ray further encouragement – in the form of a violent shove that sent him flying downwards.

Ray landed on the very platform on which the three Mounties were standing.

'Good timing,' said Frobisher as Ray and Dief landed in a winded, undignified heap. 'We could use an extra man.'

Ray looked up in utter astonishment. 'Hey! Look . . . we've just jumped into a speeding train. D'you think someone could say hello?'

'Hello Ray,' obliged Benton. Then, patting a delighted Diefenbaker on the head, he grimaced at his friend. 'We're in a bit of a pickle.'

'You're telling me,' said Ray, scrambling to his feet. 'And it's a dill.'

'C'mon then,' urged Benton. 'We've got to get to the engine room. See if we can stop this train.'

Frobisher, Ray, Benton and Dief ran hell-for-leather through the train, past the still-somnolent Mounties, the agitated horses and into the engine room. Bob Fraser didn't accompany them. Death had given him a dispensation from strenuous exercise. Wafting, now, was his thing.

'This train,' panted Ray as they entered the engine room, 'is on a collision course with a load of radioactive uranium.'

'Really?'

'Yes. They diverted it off the main track, Benny. We're now heading towards a train coming in the other direction, loaded with fuel rods. We're talking,' he added in apocalyptic tones, 'major meltdown.'

Before Benton or Frobisher could reply, a disembodied voice echoed through the engine room. Ray was the only one taken completely by surprise – the others suspected Bob Fraser. Yet when they looked round for the ghost, none was to be seen. And then the voice spoke again. It was coming, they realized, from the carriage-to-carriage intercom on the engine control panel – and it belonged to Bolt.

'We're heading south,' it crackled through the speaker.

'What do you mean, honey?' came the reply from a surprised Freya Chichester-Clark. 'I thought we were heading north.' For reasons of her own, it was imperative that she went north. Unbeknownst to Bolt, her fiancé was meeting her at a secret rendezvous from whence she would escape from Bolt with all the ransom money. She couldn't wait. Pretending to be in love with Bolt had been the most arduous part of this exercise. Still, it had kept him sweet.

'Change of plans,' was Bolt's terse reply.

'What do you mean,' piped up a third party, '"change of plans"?' The voice, thought Benton, was that of the terrorist who appeared to be called Georgie Racine.

'Well,' came the reply. 'Several changes of plan, actually. We *are* heading south, to an All Terrain Vehicle and then a helicopter. And second? Well, turns out I'm kind of greedy, so you guys won't be coming along.'

The listeners in the engine room looked at each other in silent trepidation. What on earth was going on?

Five seconds later they knew exactly what was going on. The sound of gunfire echoed clearly and sharply through the intercom, followed by a sort of slumping sound as bodies fell to the ground.

Neither Frobisher nor Bob Fraser dared look at Benton. They knew, as Ray did not, that Thatcher was with the hijackers in the caboose. She, presumably, had managed to activate the intercom. But had that been the last, heroic act of her life?

And then Bolt's voice, eerily smarmy now, wafted once again through the ether. 'Just you and me now, Inspector Thatcher.'

Ray didn't hear Benton's heartfelt sigh of relief. 'Gee!' he said, looking not entirely unhappy. 'They got the dragon lady?'

Benton ignored the remark. 'Let's get to work,' he said, turning to Frobisher.

'Alright.' Deeply grateful that Feelings appeared to be safely off the agenda, Frobisher became suddenly businesslike. 'Right. Priorities. One: defuse the train. Two: stop the bomb.'

Respectful as ever, Benton chose not to criticize. Instead, he offered an alternative. 'Or we could defuse the bomb and stop the train.'

'Exactly.' Frobisher chose not to criticize Benton for echoing his own advice. Poor boy, he thought. He's obviously distressed about the dragon lady.

'What,' frowned Benton, 'if we can't do either?'

It was Ray, staring balefully at the control panel to which the terrorists had wired the bombs, who replied. 'I've found us a safety net. There's an emergency run-off shunt a couple of miles down the line.'

'How,' asked Frobisher, 'do we pull the switch to get us on to it?'

'We don't have to,' said Ray with a broad grin. 'I've got a man on to it right now.'

'Oh?' Benton was impressed. 'Where?'

'Out there,' said Ray. 'He's got the fastest jeep in the world. He'll be at the switch before we get there.'

'Well, I sincerely hope he will be,' said Frobisher as he stepped out of the door and on to the platform at the front of the train. 'We have a train at twelve noon.'

Ray and Benton looked at each other in alarm. 'Range?' asked the latter.

It was his father, joining Frobisher on the

platform, who replied. His presence, he knew, was paramount: Buck's eyesight had never been that good, 'Six point three kilometres!' he yelled.

'Six point three kilometres!' shouted Frobisher for Ray's benefit.

Ray was horrified. 'It's gotta be sitting right in front of us!'

'Six point one kilometres!' warned the dead man.

'Six point one kilometres!' echoed the one who feared death was imminent.

'Five point seven kilometres!'

'Five point seven kilometres!'

'Where,' asked an anxious Benton, 'is your man on the shunt?'

'Don't worry,' said Ray, worrying. 'He'll be there.'

Frobisher, however, knew otherwise. He had just noticed, out of the corner of his eye, the fastest jeep in the world standing on its nose beneath an incline on the left of the train. 'No, son,' he sighed. 'I don't think he will be.' Then he turned to the younger men and, still standing on the threshold of the outside platform, drew himself up to his full height. 'Give me that gun,' he said to Benton.

'Sir?'

'You heard me. The rifle.'

Benton looked down at the rifle propped against the engine console. It had, presumably, been left by the hijackers. Perhaps, he thought, as a mocking invitation to the hostages to shoot themselves before they were melted down. Shrugging, he handed it to Frobisher. The older man, now the very picture of heroic martyrdom, stepped out on to the platform. 'Do or die,' he thought. In front of him, the train carrying the nuclear waste was speeding directly towards them. In between the two vehicles, the emergency shunt-line had come into view. Beside it was a huge, old-fashioned switch. Frobisher lifted the rifle into the crook of his shoulder. It was going to be difficult, he mused, but not impossible. The switch was a flat metal panel – one that would turn if hit by a high-velocity bullet.

'The Great Yukon Double Douglas Fir Spruce Telescoping Bank Shot?' suggested an impressed voice at his ear.

Frobisher shrugged. 'Any bloody shot I can make.' With that, he bent into firing position, only to find that the sights on the rifle defeated him. In his time, a rifle was a rifle was a rifle – no high-tech gadgetry to complicate the issue. 'Which end of this thing,' he wailed to his friend, 'do I look through?'

'Haven't a clue. Here . . .' Bob Fraser reached up, detached the sights from the weapon and threw them off the speeding train. 'How about that?'

'Much better. Modern technology,' snorted Frobisher. 'Forget it.'

Back in the engine room, Ray and Benton looked at the engine console under the supercilious gaze of

Diefenbaker. 'What,' said Ray, 'are these numbers?'

'Well . . . these indicate the hours, minutes and seconds, which means that this,' added Benton as he pointed to a different set of flickering figures, 'must indicate the . . .'

'. . . speed of the train.'

'Precisely. So the bombs will go off at the allocated time – unless the train stops. In that event, they will go off as soon as it's stationary.'

'But we don't want to stop it!'

'Yes we do, Ray. The shunt line stops after quarter of a mile.'

'Oh. But didn't you say that they'd bypassed the brakes?'

'I've just mended them.'

'Oh. How did you do that?'

'It's not important, Ray. What is important is that we must kid these instruments into thinking that the train's still moving.'

'Got you,' nodded Ray. 'Er . . . how do we do that?'

'We have to find something that's moving and connect it to the monitor.'

'Ah.' Ray looked around without much hope. Then his eyes lit up as he spotted something above them. 'How about that?'

Benton followed his gaze. 'Perfect,' he said as he saw the fan whirling round on the ceiling. 'Perfect.'

Heartily glad that they now had something to occupy their minds, both men set about dismantling the fan from its mechanism. For Ray, the activity stopped him entertaining his severe – and increasing – doubts about Frobisher's ability to shoot them on to the shunt. And as far as Benton was concerned, it stopped him thinking about something equally important – about why the intercom had gone dead.

The latter question had a simple answer. Bolt, holding Thatcher at gunpoint and with the bag of money in his other hand, had dismounted from the caboose and was running towards his next mode of transport – the all-terrain vehicle that would lead him to the helicopter hidden in a clearing in the nearby woods.

Ray's doubts over the former issue were, however, well founded.

On the platform, Frobisher shook his head and lowered the gun. 'It's an impossible angle.'

'Rubbish! No angle's impossible.'

Frobisher glared at his deceased friend. 'Look, when you made that shot you were Bob Fraser – a young Bob Fraser. Look at me now,' he said with sudden sadness. 'My eyes are fading, my knees won't hold and I've been passing wind for a week.'

Even Bob had to concede that the prognosis for a successful shot was not good. Then his eyes lit up with sudden excitement. 'Do you want me to tell you how I made that shot?'

'No.' The last thing Frobisher wanted was his friend crowing in his ear. Then, remembering they were on a bomb-laden train about to crash into another carrying lethal nuclear waste, he changed his mind. ''Course,' he said grudgingly, 'if you feel you *must*, then go ahead,'

Bob needed no further invitation. Grinning like a schoolboy, he leaned towards his friend and whispered into this ear. The last thing he wanted was eavesdroppers. He had carried the secret of that shot to his grave – and beyond. He had sworn never to divulge it to anyone else – and especially to Frobisher – yet, under the particularly challenging circumstances in which they now found themselves, he was prepared to make a gracious exception.

Whatever it was he told Frobisher, it had an immediate effect. His friend nodded several times, raised the gun once more, closed his eyes – and pulled the trigger. A moment later, a sharp 'zinging' sound echoed above the noise of the two trains as a bullet slammed into the metal switch.

'Good man,' said Bob Fraser as, in front of them, the railway tracks, protesting rustily, shifted to open the shunt line. And not a moment too soon. A few seconds later, their train thundered past the switch and on to the shunt line, its end carriage narrowly avoiding collision with the nuclear train. That train, its route now barred to it, screeched to a shuddering halt and lurched drunkenly on the axis of the shunt line.

In the engine room, Ray screamed encouragement to Benton. 'It's worked! He's done it! Hit the brakes!'

With the revolving fan now safely wired to the trigger mechanism of the bombs, Benton did as he was bid. For a moment nothing happened. Then, to their intense relief, their train began to slow down and stopped, finally, three yards from the end of the line.

Chapter Six

'If it were me, son, I'd saddle a horse.'

Still with one hand on the brake lever, Benton looked up at his father. Did he mean what he thought he meant? Was his father actually encouraging him to ride out in search of Thatcher?

As if reading his son's mind (which, given that he was dead, he probably was), Bob smiled in greater encouragement. 'Go for it, son.'

Grinning, delighting in one of their rare moments of understanding, Benton rose to his feet, squared his shoulders and strode out of the engine room.

Ray looked at him in surprise. 'Where are you going?'

'To saddle a horse.'

Baffled, Ray watched Benton's retreating figure. Typical, he thought. Not even a 'Phew, that was close.' Oh no: seconds after narrowly escaping death Benton was off again on another errand.

'Where on earth,' said Frobisher as he came in from the platform, 'is he going?'

'To saddle a horse.'

'Ah,' said the older man, breaking into a smile.

More heroics. After the successful attempt at the Great Yukon Double Douglas Fir Spruce Telescoping Bank Shot, he felt ready for anything.

'What about the men?' asked Ray.

'Yes,' said Bob Fraser. 'What about the men?'

Frobisher looked at his watch. 'Well, if Benton's right, they should be coming to right now . . .'

And as he spoke, the rousing opening bars of the second verse of the Mountie's anthem drifted towards them and the train echoed with the strains of 'Ride Forever'.

Nodding to himself, Frobisher bolted out of the engine room, leaving Ray and Diefenbaker, both suddenly forlorn. 'What's with them, Dief? Are all Mounties mad?'

But Diefenbaker didn't answer. He had witnessed the exchange between Benton and his father; knew what was about to happen. How undignified, he thought, for Benton to go chasing around the countryside after a woman – and in particular a woman like Thatcher.

But Dief's disappointment was double-edged. He had long considered himself an honorary human being, able to do everything a man could do. But no matter how honourable or honorary, there was one activity he was simply incapable of mastering.

Ray was thinking much along the same lines. 'Don't worry, Dief,' he sighed, delivering a reassuring pat on Diefenbaker's rump. 'I can't ride either.'

But the Mounties could. Invigorated by their sleep, they responded with alacrity to Benton's orders. Still singing lustily, they hurried down the carriage and into the horse cars to saddle up.

A few minutes later, the ramps of the horse cars crashed simultaneously to the ground. Had Bolt or his deceased accomplices been watching, the ensuing spectacle would have brought tears to their eyes and tingles to their spines. Thirty-four horses and thirty-four men, led by Benton and Frobisher, leaped from the train. Immaculate in red serge, battle lances at the ready and in perfect formation, they thundered across the prairie, kicking up dust in their wake as they sped off in search of their Leaderene.

The Leaderene herself was bouncing around in the passenger seat of Bolt's ATV, contemplating her fate. Why, she wondered, had he taken her with him? Would she remain a hostage forever – or would Bolt kill her as soon as he had reached freedom? If only she could *do* something . . .

But the nature of the ATV prevented her from doing anything at all except cling on for dear life. A cross between a motorbike and the sort of jeep favoured by Crew, it was hideously uncomfortable – and frighteningly fast. It was all Thatcher could do to hold on to the bar in front of her. Grinning triumphantly, Bolt had both hands on the handlebars – but his gun, tantalizingly out of reach to

Thatcher, was nestling snugly in his shoulder holster. There was absolutely nothing Thatcher could do except pray fervently to a God whom she had abandoned – in a move she now regretted – in favour of a being she had believed to be altogether more powerful. Herself.

As for Bolt, he was having the time of his life. The Mounties would be dead soon, Chicago would be panicking, his accomplices were no more – and he now had ten million dollars to call his own. What to do with them, he wondered as he charged across the rough terrain? Where to live? Whence to fly in the helicopter that he would soon reach? And what to do with his passenger? Earlier, she had irritated him by her all too obvious desire to be the centre of attention: well, now she was the centre of attention – and she didn't appear to be relishing it. Not one little bit, he saw as he cast a sidelong glance over to her. She had turned pale, her mouth was set in a thin, desperate line – but she still looked immensely sexy in her red serge.

Grinning to himself, Bolt gunned the engine and threw the little vehicle up a steep incline. By his reckoning, it was about time for the Mounties' train to collide with the one carrying nuclear waste: an explosion he just had to hear.

As he reached the top of the incline, he eased the throttle and guided the ATV to a halt. Just as he was turning to tell Thatcher to brace herself for the biggest bang of her life, he saw something strange out of the corner of his eye. It looked, he thought in one mad moment, like a forest of spindly trees on the move; Burnham Wood, to his theatrical sensibilities, on its way to Dunsinane. But as he peered into the distance, he realized, with mounting horror, exactly what the apparition was. The trees were not trees at all; they were lances. And beneath them, approaching over the horizon, were thirty-four Mounties on horseback. The Musical Ride, by some horrible twist of fate, had managed to thwart him. And now they were coming after him.

Frobisher, experiencing a second flush of youth and with it an improvement in the eyesight department, was the first to spot the ATV. He turned to Benton. 'There!' he yelled; a bellow that was swiftly followed by a word he had relished since he had first become a Mountie forty-three years previously. 'Charge!'

The Ride needed no urging. Lances lowered, the Mounties kicked their horses into a gallop and charged down the hill.

An elated Thatcher saw her chance – and then missed it. Just as she was about to dismount from the vehicle, Bolt revved the engine and screamed back the way he had come. 'Shit!' he screamed. Then he turned to his reluctant passenger. 'Why,' he snarled, 'do they always look so happy?'

Two minutes later they had reason to be happy.

An all-terrain vehicle was no match for thirty-four super-fit horses ridden by an equal number of fit men. With every second that passed, they gained ground on their quarry; and with every yard covered, they came closer to the range of their lances. At an order from Benton, they began to throw them. In a frenzied panic, Bolt tried to zig-zag around; to avoid the spikes that rained down all around him. Yet they weren't aiming for Bolt himself, but for the petrol tank on the rear of the vehicle.

Two lances punctured the tank at the same time. Thatcher let out a whoop of delight: Bolt one of despair. Then, as the vehicle started to splutter and slow down, he turned it to face the marauding army. Despite the truly awesome sight of the horses thundering towards him, he remained calm enough to reach for his holster and extract his gun. He trained it on the Mountie nearest to him – Benton.

Having missed one moment, Thatcher wasn't about to repeat the experience. In one deft movement, she snapped her elbow back, catching Bolt a heavy blow on the jaw and throwing him to the ground. Then she stood up on the vehicle and held her arms up in the air.

Benton needed no further encouragement. With hardly a break in his stride, he rode on towards the crippled ATV and, in a scene reminiscent of *Gone With The Wind* (or at least a middling-to-good

Western) he scooped Thatcher off her feet and, still without even slowing down, positioned her on the saddle behind him. As she folded her arms round his waist and held on for dear life, Thatcher experienced a fleeting moment of regret. If the film crew hadn't turned out to be terrorists, Benton's gallant rescue would have been captured forever on celluloid. There was, a healthier part of her brain told her as they galloped along, a flaw in that line of reasoning, but she couldn't for the life of her figure out what it was.

The Ride, with flawless synchronicity that would have brought tears to Commander Welsh's eyes, reconfigured itself with electrifying speed and, in one fluid movement, encircled the hapless Bolt. Lying on the ground, groping for his gun, he made a pathetic figure. His beret had fallen off, his wispy hair was straggling around his shoulders, his posturing artisan's striped Breton shirt was streaked with mud. And he was surrounded on all sides by huge whinnying horses. Yet even as he stared defeat in the face, his director's eye couldn't help admiring the fitting, theatrical nature of the denouement of the day's events. Then he remembered that he had murdered his accomplices, tried to destroy two trains and their occupants, and he began to cry.

The Ride returned to the train, still in formation

and led, on one side, by Benton and Thatcher, and on the other by Frobisher. Bolt was in the middle, doubling-up behind a particularly macho Mountie. His hands were bound and, just in case he still entertained notions of escape, the Mountie behind him held him at lance-point.

Frobisher's delight at the success of their mission was further enhanced when Bob Fraser appeared at his side. 'Say!' he exclaimed as Bob's mount fell into trotting pace with his own. 'Isn't that my old horse Bucket? The one that was shot out from under me in Dry Gulch Canyon?'

'Yes.' Bob patted the aged animal. 'Thought you'd like to see him again.'

'Yeah.' Frobisher nodded and leaned across to stroke Bucket's mane. 'Very thoughtful.'

'By the way,' said Bob. 'Did I congratulate you on that shot?'

'Not yet, no.'

'Well, it ranks right up there with the Great Yukon Double Douglas Fir Telescoping Bank Shot.'

How typical of Bob, thought Frobisher. No overt congratulations – just a backhanded compliment. 'You realize, of course,' he said with more than a tinge of superiority, 'that I knew you were always the one Caroline loved?'

'Oh.' Bob Fraser looked incensed. 'So now you're saying you missed intentionally?'

'Well,' shrugged Frobisher, 'we were friends.'

'No we weren't.'

'Yes we were.'

'Oh no.' Bob edged his horse ahead. 'No, no, no. We were not.'

Frobisher nudged his own horse forward. 'Don't you tell me that after thirty-seven years on the force . . .'

'You *told* people I was your friend.' Bob shook his head. 'But no. No, I was never your friend . . .'

And the two men continued as they had done for years, bickering into the sunset.

On the other side of the Ride, Thatcher leaned towards Benton. 'You understand, Fraser, that what happened between us can never repeat itself.' Then, regretting the statement, she inserted a let-out clause. 'Unless, of course, the exact same circumstances were to repeat themselves.'

'By exact same circumstances, sir, you mean we would have to be aboard a train loaded with unconscious Mounties that had been taken over by terrorists and was heading for a nuclear catastrophe?'

'Exactly, Fraser.'

'Understood.' Nodding and displaying no emotion whatsoever, Benton steered his mount up the last slope towards the train. He broke out into a smile as he noticed Ray was standing on the roof of the train, Diefenbaker sitting at his feet.

He wouldn't have been smiling if he knew that Diefenbaker was crying and that Ray was trying to console him. 'I know, big fellow,' said Ray as he stroked the distraught wolf. 'But there are times . . . between men and women, when things . . . come up, you know . . . Feelings.'

Diefenbaker whined in response.

'Oh well,' sighed Ray. 'Enough said.'

PART TWO

Chapter Seven

Bolt was dreaming. As dreams went, it was deeply uncreative and disappointingly reminiscent of real life. It started with him filming a troupe of Mounties embarking on their historic Musical Ride, continued with him gassing the occupants of a train and threatening to blow up Chicago unless he was paid ten million dollars – and went on to encompass a nuclear threat. After that it turned rather sour and saw him being thwarted by the troupe of Mounties and ending up in jail. It wasn't, all in all, a particularly satisfactory dream, and a part of Bolt's subconscious urged him to wake up, forget about all the unpleasantness, and seize the day with a joyous vigour.

The problem, however, was that when Bolt woke up it was with the realization that he had recently been thwarted in his grandiose plan to blow up Chicago and steal ten million dollars and was, as a result, in jail. Not good.

The nasty, dark little cell in which the waking-up occurred had been Bolt's home for the last month: a month comprising twenty-eight days – on each of which Bolt had been visited by the dream. This day, the twenty-ninth of his incarceration while he awaited trial, was to see a different and altogether more welcome type of visit. This Bolt knew when the guard appeared at his cell, whacked the iron bars with his nightstick and announced that 'You've got a visitor.'

Still unhappily sweaty from the dream, Bolt rolled off the bed and blinked in surprise. 'A visitor?' Then his face darkened. 'I'm handling my own defence,' he growled, 'so if it's that no-account lawyer you can feed him to the pigs while his bones are still soft.'

The guard, who would have given his right arm to feed Bolt to the pigs, snorted his response. 'It's your brother.'

'Ah.' Bolt smiled broadly, a smile that would have passed for beatific had Bolt been more attractive. The guard shuddered and unlocked the cell door. 'My brother,' sighed Bolt. 'Different story, morning glory.'

The guard shuddered again as Bolt passed into the corridor towards the visiting area. Bolt was one of his least favourite inmates and he couldn't wait to see the back of him. But as he followed the prisoner up the corridor, he realized he had something to be thankful for. Bolt might be strange, but the brother who was waiting to see him was surely certifiable.

Francis Bolt knew differently. He knew he was a genius: infinitely superior to the rest of mankind;

possessed of a towering and mathematically-inclined intellect that could provide an answer to any problem. He was currently addressing that intellect to the problem of springing his brother from jail. It was, he had recently decided, hardly a problem at all.

Francis smiled to himself as he waited for his brother. The prison guard standing beside him found that smile particularly chilling: it somehow made no difference to the strange, expressionless face or to the button-like eyes that stared unblinking from behind the little round glasses. More strangely, it didn't cause any movement in the grim little moustache cowering on his upper lip. Yuk, thought the guard.

Francis thought much the same when his brother appeared. Randall looked positively dirty and his hair – Francis was meticulous about hair – was wispy, too long and unkempt. 'You need a haircut, Randall,' he said by way of greeting.

'Well,' smirked his brother as he sat down on the opposite chair, 'at least I've still got most of mine, Bro.' Randall looked at the shiny pate above the little round glasses. A skating rink for flies, he had once called it. Francis hadn't found that remotely amusing but, given that Francis had no discernible sense of humour, that hadn't been surprising.

Francis sighed and held up an admonitory hand. 'Don't start, Randall.'

'Look – my hair-do is the least of my problems.'

'Still, you shouldn't let hygiene take a back seat.'

'I'm in prison, Francis!'

But the cold, clinical and scrupulously clean Francis Bolt wasn't impressed. 'Hygiene is important, Randall.'

Bolt rolled his eyes. 'I could be facing a lethal injection here.'

At that, Francis smiled again. 'Oh, I don't think so.'

'You don't think so?' Bolt stared, aghast, across the table. 'I got a hanging judge out there, Francis! He's filling up that big needle right now, getting ready to send me off to my final reward, don't you think?'

Francis leaned forward. 'No. No, I don't think that.'

'And why is that, Francis?'

'Because . . . the family would never permit it.'

To the guards standing close to the brothers, the word 'family' seemed innocuous enough. After all, everyone had a family, didn't they? Even people like these. But to Randall Bolt, the word was highly significant. The Bolt family had Mafia-like tendencies – and with them tentacles in every criminal pie. Several of them were murderers, some of them were bank robbers – and the majority of them were, like Randall, extremely handy with explosives. All of them belonged to the Fathers of the Confederation supremacist group. Most of them, however, were rather more successful than Randall in their chosen careers. He, they had sadly realized, was something of a black sheep. To have been discharged from the army for blowing up an officers' mess had been merely unfortunate; to have subsequently failed as both a film director and a terrorist was verging on the dishonourable. But to have ended up in jail was simply not on: none of the family had ever been to jail. 'Mother' was mortified.

'Ah,' sighed Randall, 'the family.'

'As you know,' continued his brother, 'the family is dedicated to your cause.' This, he knew, was pushing things a bit. Some members had been a bit shirty about helping Francis extract Randall from his present predicament. Still, they had eventually come round and were, as the brothers talked, preparing for his release.

'Even now,' said Francis, 'we're preparing a care package for the day of your trial.'

A care package. Randall was impressed. In family shorthand that meant a larger than average bomb. And 'the day of the trial' was even more interesting. That meant they were going to spring him from the court room, not the jail itself. 'Ah. Good,' he said, noting with relief that the guards were blissfully unaware of the information they were exchanging. 'What about the cousins,' he asked. 'They still behind me?'

'They always have been,' reproached Francis. 'Do you recall the games we used to play at Uncle Jimmy's mortuary?'

'They weren't games, Francis.' Randall looked upset. 'They pickled my dogs.'

Francis waved a dismissive hand. 'Let the dogs go, Randall.'

'But they weren't even dead!'

'Let them go, I say. Think instead,' he added with an encouraging smile, 'of Dracula.'

'Dracula?'

'Exactly.'

'Ah.' Suddenly Randall understood. More shorthand. 'You mean,' he asked to make sure he was on the right track, 'the time the cousins hid themselves in the coffins?'

One of the guards, overhearing the macabre remark, wrinkled his nose in disgust. No wonder these two were so strange.

But the guard, of course, wasn't privy to the Bolt brothers' secret code; he had no way of knowing that 'hiding in coffins' meant installing yourself in armaments crates at a U.S. Army Weapons Depot ready to filch masses of hardware. Big bangs were planned, thought an impressed Randall. Suddenly aware that the guard on his left was looking at them with extreme distaste, he sought to lighten the conversation. 'How's Vern's asthma, by the way?'

'Well,' shrugged Francis, 'he still suffers . . . but

the attacks are bearable.'

Randall nodded in sympathy. The words confirmed that Vern was the one looting the weapons. Which meant, usually, that Gabe would be with him . . . 'What about Gabe,' he enquired. 'He and Vern still close?'

'Like peas in a pod. Of course,' added Francis with regret, 'he still has his problems. It seems that on occasion he finds himself incapable of resisting the urge to get loaded.'

Randall nodded in sympathy.

'And lately,' continued Francis, 'he's developed a taste for things that are somewhat more dangerous.'

Oh goody, thought Randall. That means we're planning something really big. Not just my escape, but lots of other things as well. Holding the entire courtroom hostage, maybe? Blowing up the judge? Threatening to destroy the entire courthouse unless they were paid lots of lovely money? The possibilities were endless – if a little reminiscent of the unhappy events on the train that had led to his incarceration. 'Well,' he said as he leaned back in his chair, 'this news of the family is all very encouraging, Francis.'

'Very encouraging,' smiled his brother, emphasizing the 'very'.

'And encouragement, said Randall, 'is just what I need, 'cos right now I've been having the devil of a time in here.' He turned and grinned at the scowling guards. 'Right fellas?'

The guards, being blissfully unaware of the significance of the word 'devil', continued to scowl.

'It's interesting,' said Francis, 'that you should speak of the Devil. Our father was at the pulpit last Sunday... God decided to show him a vision. He showed him the face of Satan.'

Ah, so killing *is* involved, thought Randall. 'What,' he asked, leaning forward again, 'does Satan look like?'

'Well, the curious thing, from a theological standpoint, is that Satan has two faces.' With that, Francis delved into his breast pocket and produced two photographs. One of the guards, seeing the movement, sprang forward. 'Hey...!'

'They're only family snaps,' protested Francis.

'Oh yeah, right.' Lip curling, the guard surveyed the two brothers. 'Of Dracula and Satan and the rest. Nice family.'

'I take it,' said Francis with sanctimonious piety, 'you don't share our family's religious fervour?'

'Too right.' The guard stepped back as Francis pushed the photographs through the glass partition.

Randall Bolt's eyes widened as he looked at the 'family snaps'.

'Well,' he said. 'As Father says, "a man cannot be free until he erases his mistakes".' Then he looked down again at the two photographs. One was of Benton Fraser; the other of Ray Vecchio. Both mistakes. Both had been mistakes. Both had to be erased.

Chapter Eight

Many people held varied and sometimes conflicting views about Benton. Mad, Bad and Dangerous to Know was the one favoured by Ray, while others veered from the saintly to the simply insane. There was, however, one aspect of Benton's character on which everyone agreed – his innate modesty. Even those who disliked him (and those people were all on the wrong side of a cell door) concurred that the last thing in the world he would ever do was crow about his achievements or his abilities. He just didn't crave fame or adulation.

To most Americans, this modesty was incomprehensible. How could someone so heroic, so good-looking and so disarmingly well-mannered not want to be a national hero? How could he possibly pass up the chance to host his own chat show, to appear in television adverts for dog food – to be considered as the latest hero in a new epic TV movie about swashbuckling (the producers were still a bit iffy about what swashbuckling entailed)? Why, for heaven's sake, didn't he want to be *famous*?

The television producer standing in front of him

in the Canadian Consulate in Chicago was one of those Americans. Modesty, she wanted to scream, is a *crime*! No decent person ever got anywhere by being self-effacing. She wanted to shake him; to tell him he was a national hero and that the world, in consequence, was his oyster.

She had no way of knowing that Benton hated oysters.

'Alright,' she said, motioning for the cameras to stop rolling. 'Let's try again.' Stepping forward, she adjusted the RCMP crest in the wall behind Benton, dabbed at his forehead (unnecessarily – but a touch was a touch) with her make-up and wondered, not for the first time, if this report on a true-life drama was going to break her career. Initially, she had been confident it was going to make it. Her first glimpse of Benton had turned that confidence into conviction. *Nobody* would be able to resist this Mountie.

Thatcher, sitting opposite Benton at the end of the conference room, had, of course, recently experienced the fruits of irresistibility. She didn't for a moment regret what she had now come to call The Moment, but its consequence was that she was hyper-aware that others – this power-suited minx with the big hair, for example – wanted to have a bit of Moment as well.

Vivian Richards – for the minx was she – was now ready for her next take. She smiled, seductively she was sure, at Benton and thrust the microphone between them. 'Constable Fraser,' she announced in breathy tones, 'you're on a train loaded with explosives, full of Royal Canadian Mounted Policemen, and you are headed towards a nuclear disaster and you avert that disaster. How does that make you feel?'

'Feel?'

Vivian Richards nodded. 'Feel.'

'Fine,' said Benton with a shrug.

Vivian took a deep breath. Just as well, she told herself, that this wasn't a live broadcast. It was proving to be *very* uphill work. Were she not so experienced and so professional, she reckoned she might lose her temper. Just as well, she reminded herself, she didn't fancy the hunky Mountie – or else she might begin to go off him. And just as well he appeared not to be too interested in women – or else she might be jealous of the hard-faced, pink-suited but admittedly rather attractive harridan at the other end of the table.

'Cut!' screamed Vivian. Then, remembering that she never lost her temper, she took another deep breath. 'Constable,' she said, mustering a smile. 'I'd like you to imagine a spotlight – a big spotlight – and it is focused on you. You are the centre of a media frenzy which we are trying to capitalize on.' To illustrate the point, she stepped forward and opened the door, revealing an ante-room full of frenzied journalists. 'Take a look,' she urged Benton, 'at these people.'

Benton took a look. The sight was anathema to him. Hordes of people looking for their fifteen minutes of fame by trying to interview somebody else about their own fifteen minutes.

Suddenly aware that her own quarter-hour was in jeopardy, Vivian slammed the door shut again, boffing a particularly persistent news hound on the nose. Then she turned back to Benton. 'You are,' she explained, 'already on their television sets and on the covers of their magazines. But they want *more*. They want your inner soul. Think *Roseanne*,' she implored. 'Show 'em your scars.'

Benton looked, perplexed, at the woman in front of him. Wasn't she supposed to be an expert media advisor as well as a television producer? 'With respect, ma'am, I thought it was our unstated protocol to avoid the appearance of currying favour with the media.'

'We sold out to Disney, Constable,' snapped Vivian. 'That is about as curried as it gets now. You really are going to have to trust me on this. I am an expert,' she lied, 'on RCMP media relations and I'd like us to focus on the details.' Sighing again, she glanced down at the clipboard in her left hand. 'Okay . . . I want you to tell us how you got from the horse carriage to the engine room.'

'Ah.' Benton looked down the room towards his

superior officer. She looked back, her face an inscrutable mask. Behind the mask, her soul was aglow. 'Well,' began Benton, 'I followed Inspector Thatcher up the ladder. Then we ran along the top of the train. Inspector Thatcher stopped, turned . . . we engaged in a conversation.' Looking straight at Vivian, Benton was unaware that Thatcher had turned a deathly shade of pale. Unaware, too, that she was mouthing 'stop' noises.

'It was a conversation,' continued Benton in a somewhat strangled voice, 'that led to us discovering ourselves . . .'

'Constable!' shrieked Thatcher, jumping to her feet. 'That was terrific. Bravo. A marked improvement, But,' she added as she brushed past the big-haired minx, 'could I have a word with you?'

'By all means.' Benton turned to an intrigued Vivian, muttered an 'excuse me' and accompanied Thatcher to the other end of the room.

'Fraser,' she said as soon as they were out of earshot. 'Our, um . . . what would be the word for it?'

'Contact?' suggested Benton, after a moment's thought.

'Contact. Yes. That's a very good word. Our "contact", in my opinion, is not something that is needing to be aired.'

Benton nodded. 'And since it had no impact on the outcome of the event, I agree. Furthermore, sir,

I followed your instructions and I've tried to erase the . . . the "contact" from my memory.'

'You have?' Thatcher was not in the habit of emitting indignant squeaks. This time, however, she couldn't stop herself.

'Yes.'

A glint came into Thatcher's eye. 'And have you succeeded?'

For the sake of professional decorum, Benton desperately wanted to say 'yes.' Lies, however, did not come easily to him. 'No,' he admitted.

The glint left Thatcher's eyes. For a moment, both of them felt as if they were back on the roof of the train; about to fall into each other's arms; on the point of . . .

But instead they were interrupted by Constable Cooper, carrying a tray of coffee.

'Ah!' said Thatcher, springing away from Benton with guilty and unseemly alacrity. 'We were just . . . just . . .'

Cooper, however, was as ungifted in the observation department as he was in the intellectual one. His great redeeming feature, in Thatcher's eyes (she had employed him before the 'contact') was that he was both jolly good-looking and terribly afraid of Thatcher. 'Sorry to interrupt,' he said, not taking his eyes off his tray, 'but I have the coffee and I also have the java tea and . . . Oh Holy Moly!' Cooper looked at Thatcher with the sort of pained anguish more suited to bereavement. 'I've forgotten the sweetener. If you could give me a couple of ticks, I'll be right back.' Without waiting for Thatcher's reply (normally it was a variation on the theme of 'you're fired'), he fled. Unfortunately, his flight took him into the wrong room: the one filled with frenzied reporters.

'Constable!' shouted the woman whose nose – and possibly career – had been damaged by Vivian Richards' door-slamming pursuit of fame. 'If I could ask you just one question?'

'I'm sorry,' replied the contrite constable. 'I forgot the sweetener.'

'Just one question!'

Head bowed, Cooper tried to barge his way through the throng. 'I have no comment. No comment at all.'

Tracey Wightman dabbed at her damaged nose and indulged in a little internal fuming. What was it with these Canadians, she wondered? Why were they all so shy? How could they possibly say 'no comment' when half of America wanted to hang on to their every word? One tiny admission – and who cared if it wasn't true? – could lead to a movie deal.

And then Tracey Wightman spotted, battling his way in the direction of the conference room, someone who looked vaguely familiar. Her spirits soared. Tracey knew that anyone who appeared familiar to her must, *per se*, be famous. An ambitious girl, she never bothered acquainting herself with people who were not, or were not likely to become, famous. Beckoning to her film crew, Tracey shot towards the newcomer. Stopping him dead in his tracks, she shoved her microphone in his face. 'Who are you with?' she yelled. This was Tracey's stock opening line. It was, she felt, nicely open-ended; not too intrusive.

Incensed at being assaulted – and particularly by a woman with a nose like an aubergine – Ray Vecchio adopted his most supercilious sneer. '*With?*' he drawled. 'Who am I with? I'm with me.' Ray tapped his chest to illustrate the point. 'Ray Vecchio, the guy who saved Illinois.'

Tracey almost fainted. 'Are you the detective that was on the train?'

Ray drew himself to his full height. 'I wasn't just *on* the train, baby. I *stopped* the train.'

This didn't quite square with Tracey's view of the world. In her book, it was always the good-looking one who saved the day and there was no way this detective was even half as attractive as the Mountie. Still, a balding detective with a big nose was better than no hero at all. 'Can I please,' she began as she beckoned her film crew, 'have a few words?'

'Sure,' preened Ray.

'Are we rolling?' Tracey asked the cameraman.

'Rolling.'

'Right.' Fixing the camera with her best anchor-woman smile (but forgetting about the aubergine above it), she began her impassioned, breathy report. 'I am standing now with someone who was actually on the train. Detective Vecchio – answer me just one question?'

Ray smiled for the benefit of his public. 'Go ahead.'

'So, what's the Mountie like?' The question succeeded where even the hardest of slaps might have failed: Ray's smile vanished. It was replaced, briefly, by a flash of anger and then . . . by nothing. Like the smile, Ray vanished.

'Detective!' screamed Tracey. 'Detective Vecchio . . . !' But it was no use; a po-faced Ray was already pushing his way into the conference room, thereby depriving Tracey of her scoop and, probably, a promotion.

Ray had not been having the jolliest of times since the episode on the train. This was largely because the public at large shared Tracey Wightman's view that Benton, being both very good-looking and a Mountie, must have been the saviour of both the day and of Chicago. Nobody had given Ray any credit for his role in the rescue. No one had applauded his daring leap on to the moving train; not a soul had commended him on his bravery. Even Welsh, while secretly delighted that it had been Benton and Ray and not the FBI who had thwarted Bolt, had reprimanded Ray for taking matters into his own hands and disobeying orders.

'*Orders?*' Ray had been horrified by the accusation. His orders, as far as he had been concerned, had ended with hanging the money on the mail pole. After that, he had been free to do as he liked.

'Yes.' Miffed that the RCMP and not the Chicago police were getting the credit for the affair, Welsh had to let his anger out on someone. 'Your orders,' he thundered, 'stopped with hanging the money on the mail post.'

'Exactly, sir. After that I used my initiative to stop the train.'

'The FBI and the media would appear to disagree with you on that one, Vecchio. "Runaway Train Stopped by Detective's Initiative" is a headline I have yet to read.'

Accustomed to being on the delivering rather than the receiving end of sarcasm, Ray found himself at a loss for words. Welsh wasn't. He ended the conversation with a curt 'dismissed'.

Ray was again at a loss for words when he entered the conference room at the Canadian consulate. He waited patiently while Vivian Richards ran through – yet again – her questions with Benton and while Benton steadfastly refused to be immodest with his answers.

'Hello, Ray,' said Benton when the interview was

finished and Thatcher and Vivian Richards had departed.

'I'm not talking to you,' snarled Ray.

'Oh. Why's that?' Benton had been slightly worried about Ray of late. For his friend to be subdued was unusual: for him to be silent was distinctly alarming. Not, strictly speaking, that he was being completely silent. 'I'm not talking to you' counted, after all, as talking. Benton thought it best not to mention that at the moment.

'I'm just not talking to you,' replied Ray.

'Oh.' Then Benton remembered why Ray was here. 'But you said you'd give me a lift home.'

'I know. That's why I'm here.'

'Oh. Well. . . Shall we go?'

Ray nodded.

This, thought Benton as they left the consulate and headed to Ray's car, was all extremely peculiar. Why, today of all days, was Ray choosing to be uncommunicative? 'Look, Ray,' he said as he eased himself into the passenger seat of the Riviera, 'just so I can be really clear in my own mind; other than telling me that you're not talking, you are, in fact, really not talking. The only talking you're doing is telling me you're not talking, right?'

Ray gunned the engine and shot down the street with more urgency than was necessary – or indeed legal. 'That,' he growled, 'is about the size of it.'

'I see. Look,' added Benton after a short and

uncomfortable silence, 'is there something I should know?'

'There is.'

Another silence.

'Well,' suggested an increasingly perplexed Benton. 'This thing I should know. Do you think you could perhaps provide me with a hint as to what it might be?'

'Alright.' Mouth set in a thin, angry line, Ray reached forward into the glove compartment, extracted a magazine and threw it across to Benton.

How on earth, thought a surprised Benton, could a magazine possibly make Ray so angry? He never read anything in magazines; only looked at the pictures.

But some pictures could tell a story – and the picture on the front cover of America's largest-circulation glossy magazine told a very fine story indeed. It even painted a thousand words – handily removing the necessity of opening the magazine to read those words. That picture was a large and extremely flattering photograph of Benton.

'Ah,' said Benton, embarrassed. 'Well . . . I suppose I should probably just . . .'

'Get out of my car.'

Benton was horrified. 'But I thought you said you'd give me a lift home?'

'You are home.'

Benton looked out the window. 'Oh. So I am. That was quick.'

'Yeah. So maybe you can be just as quick about getting out of my car.'

Benton was now truly astounded. Ray, he well knew, was prone to extreme over-reactions – but this was the most extreme Benton had ever witnessed. He really didn't know how to deal with it. And then he looked at Ray and realized the best way was to reach for the handle, open the door and get out of the car. Quickly. 'Er . . . thank you Ray,' he said as he exited the vehicle.

Ray's only reply was to slam his foot down on the accelerator and scream off down the street.

Somewhat depressed, but trying to rationalize the situation, Benton made his way to his apartment. The present situation would, he knew, soon belong to the past – but for the first time since he had known Ray, Benton was beginning to wonder if their friendship would also take on a historical aspect.

Ray was wondering the same thing. By the time he let himself into his own apartment, he had verbalized that wondering. 'This,' he said as he walked through the kitchen and opened the fridge, 'is ridiculous.' An onlooker (had there been one) would have faced a multiple choice as to exactly what he was referring. Was it a) the fact that he was talking to himself, b) the fact that the fridge was empty save for a jar of mouldy pickles, or, c) the fact that he was being petty about Benton's new-found but not sought-after fame?

Ray himself was not entirely sure of the answer. He did, however, continue talking: a) as an alternative to eating mouldy pickles and b) as an outlet for his anger, jealousy and depression. 'We put that guy behind bars,' he said, 'he's ready to go to trial . . . and now I walk into that room today and this little bouncy reporter comes up to me and I'm thinking "alright, Ray, here's your chance. Here's a little reward for putting yourself in harm's way one more time." And,' he continued as he paced the room, 'what's the first question she asks me?' Shaking his head in outraged disbelief, he repeated Tracey Wightman's question. ' "So what's the Mountie like?" '

Letting the upsetting nature of the question sink into his audience – the fridge – Ray paused for a short, dramatic moment. 'Well,' he sneered at the non-committal Electrolux, 'he's superman, alright? That's what you want me to say, isn't it? But he's really a moron. He dresses up in that damn uniform every single day of his life. Looks like a signpost.'

Ray would have been intrigued to know that Benton, pacing up and down the kitchen of his own apartment several blocks away, was also talking to himself, trying to rationalize Ray's depression, anger and jealousy; wondering if he had unconsciously tried to foster those feelings.

'Is it the uniform?' he asked aloud. His audience – Diefenbaker – made no response. Like Ray's fridge, he maintained a frosty silence. Unlike the fridge, however, he was sulking. Benton had forgotten to feed him.

'Well, let me tell you,' continued Benton, 'the truth is there are times when I wish I didn't have to wear it. I mean, the thing itches . . . it itches three hundred and sixty-five days of the year – unless, of course, it's a leap year, in which case it itches for three hundred and sixty-six days. But the point is,' he explained, 'I don't wear it intentionally. It's part of my obligations.'

On the other side of town, Ray had moved on from the uniform and had become more personal in his assassination of his friend. He was busy explaining to the fridge that Benton was, in fact, the most irritating man in the world.

Benton knew Ray felt this and, on his side of the Windy City, was addressing that very issue. 'I know I irritate you,' he said as he paced, 'but you have to believe me – I'm not *trying* to irritate you. It's not part of some sort of master plan. You know, the fact of the matter is, I often try to imagine how you would handle a given situation. The other day, for instance, I saw this woman who was in a wheelchair and she was having difficulty with a set of doors. I was about to help her when all of a sudden I just heard your voice in my head . . . and do you know what you were saying?' Given that Ray was several miles away, this was highly unlikely. It didn't, however, stop Benton enlightening him. 'You were saying "Hey, Fraser, what the hell's wrong with you? Why do you feel duty bound to help every single cripple in the greater Chicago area? What the hell do you think they have those handicap buttons for?"' Benton paused again and stared at the increasingly exasperated Diefenbaker. 'And do you know something, Ray? You were right. I'm always trying to help people and I shouldn't . . . and if I needed any proof of that I got it when I helped the lady into a cab which promptly ran over my foot . . . But the point, you see, of the anecdote is that while I was helping her, I knew that you would be irritated with me and I'm sorry. I seem to be powerless to help that. I don't know,' he said, more to himself than to the absent Ray, 'maybe it's some sort of flaw in my upbringing. Some genetic abnormality. Or maybe,' he mused, casting his mind back to his birthplace, 'maybe it's just some sort of aberrant property in the Tuktoyuktuk water system.'

Ray, however, wasn't able to enlighten Benton as to the origin of the flaw in Benton's personality. He was too busy accusing Benton – alias the fridge – about his most irritating fault: his inability to express emotion. 'It's human to express emotion,

Fraser!' he yelled at the unsuspecting fridge. 'Are you a human? Because if you are, human beings *feel* things, okay? They feel anger, they feel love, they feel lust and fear. And sometimes, Fraser – and I know you don't want to hear this – sometimes they even cry.'

Ray would have been extremely surprised, and not a little gratified to know that Benton, at that very moment, was looking distinctly dewy-eyed. He was also feeling something; a human emotion; a deep concern that he might lose his best friend.

Then something extremely peculiar happened – in both apartments. It was the sort of thing that, had either man had time to think about it, would look terrific on TV. There was a knock on Benton's front door: there was a knock on Ray's front door. Benton opened the door and was overjoyed to see Ray: Ray opened his door and was overjoyed to see Benton. Each man let the other into his apartment – and then each man knocked the other out cold with a hefty punch.

Even those who believe that truth is stranger than fiction would be pretty hard-pressed to swallow that one. Cries of 'impossible!' would ring out, and the odd rotten tomato would be hurled. But then they would find themselves looking foolish when given the explanation of the scenario.

For the man who knocked Benton to the ground was wearing a lifelike latex mask of Ray's face –

and the man who delivered the blow to Ray was sporting a mask of Benton. And those men, when they peeled off their masks, revealed themselves to be none other than Vern and Gabe – 'cousins' to the murderous Bolt brothers.

Chapter Nine

An hour after the nifty ploy that felled the two faces of Satan, Ray was – and this really *is* true this time – at Benton's apartment. He had been brought there by Vern, his assailant, and had been placed, to the chagrin of his unconscious mind, in a rolled-up Persian carpet in the centre of the room.

Benton's position was equally undignified. After flooring him, Gabe had tied him to a chair, wherein he was currently slumped. He was also rather wet, having just had a bucket of freezing water thrown in his face to wake him up. The sight that greeted him when he lurched back into the land of the living sent a tremor of fear (a human emotion!) down his spine. Diefenbaker was lying unconscious in the corner of the room.

But Benton had no time to ponder his pet's state of health. The second sight that met his eyes was equally alarming: the cold, clinical face of Francis Bolt as he leaned towards him.

'That's a fine animal,' said Francis in, for a terrorist, a surprisingly drinks-party sort of way. 'Fifty per cent wolf, if I'm not mistaken.'

'What,' mumbled Benton, 'have you done to him?'

'Oh, he's alright. He'll wake up soon.' Then Francis leaned closer and pressed his unpleasant face rather closer to Benton's than a drinks party would have tolerated. 'Please answer the question,' he snarled.

Given that Benton had been unconscious when Francis had posed the question, he was not best equipped to answer it. 'Er . . . what question?'

'The one I just asked you.'

'I'm terribly sorry, but I didn't actually hear it. I was unconscious, you see. Your friend over there,' Benton nodded towards Gabe, 'hit me. I thought he was *my* friend, but of course he was wearing a mask modelled on Ray's face and . . .'

'Shut up!'

'Yes. Sorry.' Benton had just noticed what Gabe, assisted by Vern, was doing: he was painstakingly constructing a bomb on Benton's kitchen table. The prognosis, thought Benton, was not good. Under the circumstances, shutting up was probably the best idea.

'I was asking you,' said Francis, 'if you know who I am?'

'No. No. I'm afraid I can't place you.'

Francis subjected Benton to the horrid little leer that was his version of a smile. 'Well, I know all about you. I even know the story of how you came to have a wolf as a pet. I know that it happened in mid-May, two hundred and twelve miles northwest of Whitehorse in the Yukon Territories . . .' Francis paused. 'Sorry,' he said after a frowning hesitation, 'is that Territor*ies* or Territor*y*?'

'Territory.'

'Thank you, I crave accuracy. Now then, as I was saying . . . I know that your wolf – Diefenbaker, isn't it? – saved you when you were stuck on an ice-floe, that you subsequently saved him and then rescued him from starvation, and that you have been together ever since.'

A faint bell began to ring in the back of Benton's mind. The story was true – and he had encountered its teller before. There was something vaguely familiar about the chilling voice, and the mention of a craving for accuracy . . .

'I know a lot more,' continued Francis, 'but I suspect you're beginning to remember who I am. Do you know – or shall I go on?'

'No . . . no, I remember.' Benton closed his eyes, willing back the memory. 'Yes, I think I can. Your name,' he sighed, 'would be Francis Bolt. You were born in Oregon in 1949 . . .'

'. . . 1950,' corrected Francis, wincing at the inaccuracy of Benton's recollection.

'Sorry. 1950. You are a theoretical mathematician by training and a recluse by choice. And,' continued Benton, now aware of why he and Ray had been attacked, 'you have a younger brother named Randall.'

147

'Yes.' Francis leered again. 'Who you arrested. That,' he said, wagging a finger, 'was a mistake.'

'He killed several people and tried to cause a nuclear disaster. And he tried to steal ten million dollars.' Benton held his head high. 'I would arrest him again in a heartbeat.'

'You would?' Francis aimed an angry kick at the Persian carpet. In response, it unravelled to reveal the bound, gagged and indignantly conscious Ray. 'Detective Vecchio?' Francis leaned down and ripped the gag from Ray's mouth. 'I'd like it if you could talk your friend over there into apologizing for arresting my brother.'

'Well, you're out of luck, pal,' snarled Ray. 'I'm not talking to him.'

If Bolt was taken aback by the reply, he hid his surprise behind his death's head countenance. 'My brother's problem,' he said, 'is the same. But then geniuses are plagued by problems.'

'Yeah?' sneered Ray. 'Like not being able to get a date?' Ray was feeling thoroughly out of sorts. Still, at least there was a rightness, a certain symmetry about what was happening. If Benton hadn't been such a hero, then Benton wouldn't be in his current, compromising situation. It hadn't yet dawned on Ray that he was in exactly the same position.

'You,' said Francis, pointing with a bony, almost skeletal finger, 'are a wisecracker, Detective, whereas I am a mathematician. I look for symmetry, for order within chaos. Let us take, for example, the charter train, coded 56032. I was the mastermind behind that plan. You; you are here to account for your part in thwarting that plan.'

Belatedly, it dawned on Ray that he was in exactly the same boat as Benton. He was lying, ignominiously bound, on a Persian carpet (but at least it was Persian); he was in the presence of what appeared to be a madman. Furthermore, there were two other men in the room – and they appeared to be busily manufacturing bombs. Not a happy situation.

'That plan,' continued Francis, 'was rigorous in its detail. And as a wise man once said, "God is in the details." So,' he finished, dripping piety, 'it is to God that you both now will answer.'

Ray and Benton exchanged unhappy, slightly fearful looks. Maniacs were dangerous enough; religious ones were, on balance, infinitely worse.

'My brother's trial,' announced Francis as he moved over the bomb-making table, 'is tomorrow.'

'We know that,' said Ray before he could help himself.

Francis ignored him. 'Tonight, you will both stay here.'

'Figured that,' muttered Ray.

'And in the morning . . . well, do you know what you will be doing in the morning?'

Neither Benton nor Ray liked the tone of Francis's voice; the expression that suggested a fate worse than death. They remained silent.

And then Francis decreed that fate. 'You will be wearing Mexican ponchos.'

Chapter Ten

The media had been anticipating Randall Bolt's trial with great glee. No one, of course, was much interested in Bolt himself, and while the charges against him – two of murder, one of attempted murder, one of possession and transportation of explosives with intent to commit a felony, one of grand theft, one of hijacking, thirty-two of assault and one of intent to overthrow the United States Government – were indeed newsworthy, they were not quite as sensational as that other element of the case: Constable Benton Fraser's heroic involvement.

But when the court convened on the appointed morning, Constable Benton Fraser was heroically absent. Resplendent in her red serge, Thatcher stood outside the twelve-storey courthouse until the last moment, scanning the street for a breathless, belated Mountie. Her scanning, however, was in vain.

The Assistant State Attorney, pointedly looking at his watch, sidled up to her. 'We're getting down to the wire here, Inspector. Only minutes to go. Where on earth is he?'

'I don't know,' snapped Thatcher.

The Attorney recoiled as if he had been hit. He had forgotten, temporarily, about Inspector Thatcher's fearsome reputation. 'Well,' he said, meekly contrite, 'I . . . I think it would be best if we went in. The bailiff's already reading the charges. We don't want to miss the trial altogether.'

Imperious in her anger, Thatcher swept past him. The sweeping motion also involved passing the security guard, at whom she didn't even deign to look. Had she done so, she would have noticed that the guard was none other than cousin Gabe. On the other hand, having never met Gabe before, his face would have meant nothing to her. A pity, really, in the light of what was about to happen.

In the lobby of the courthouse, Thatcher headed for the bank of payphones. Again she swept, this time past Vern, also dressed as a security guard. Unnoticed by her, he was in the process of clearing two large bags through the X-ray machine. The delicious irony, to the man who lurked in the corner of the lobby, was that one of the bags contained the very person Thatcher was looking for. The lurking man was Francis Bolt and the person, of course, was Benton.

The criminal population of the courthouse could have told Thatcher that her phonecall to Benton's apartment, followed by another frantic one to his neighbour, would be in vain. Benton was not at home, and Mr Mustafi, while in residence, refused point-blank to cross the hallway. 'Too dangerous,' he said down the line before slamming the phone down on Thatcher. Worried now as well as angry, Thatcher made her way into the courtroom.

'Let it be duly noted,' the judge was saying as she entered, 'that defense waives its right to an opening statement.' Then, turning to address the prosecution, he nodded to Delia Sheldrake, the State Attorney. 'The State will now call its first witness, please.'

Delia stood up. 'Thank you, Your Honour. The State,' she announced with somewhat unprofessional pride and a huge smile, 'calls Constable Benton Fraser.'

The State, however, was to be thwarted. The Assistant Attorney, following Thatcher into the courtroom, rushed up to Delia and whispered in her ear. Above them, Judge Brock looked on in irritation. He prided himself on the smoothness of the trials over which he presided. Urgent whisperings caused delays and were to be discouraged. 'Is there a problem, Ms Sheldrake?'

Delia, now with two unbecoming pink spots in her cheeks, looked up to the bench. 'It would appear, Your Honour, that Constable Fraser has been delayed. Perhaps I could maybe . . .'

'Perhaps you could do what?' snapped Brock. 'We've barely got our toes in the pond and you've lost your first witness? This does not inspire confidence on the bench, Councillor.'

Delia appeared to be in danger of withering. This was her first major trial, and already it was collapsing around her. 'I understand that, Your Honour,' she said valiantly. 'However, I had anticipated that this witness's testimony would cover the bulk of today and . . .'

'You should invest in a calendar, Councillor. You'd be surprised at how much time you've had to prepare for this case.'

Ouch, thought Delia. 'I am aware,' she protested, 'of the time I've had to prepare . . .'

'Well,' interrupted Brock, looking at his watch, 'if your witness does not appear pronto . . .'

At that precise moment, the doors opened. An expectant hush descended in the courtroom. And then the witness appeared. The reporters in the press gallery gasped as they took in the sight before them. Constable Benton Fraser was clad in an oversized Mexican poncho: beside him, also inside the poncho, was Detective Ray Vecchio. Seemingly joined at the hip, they shuffled into the middle of the room.

Delia was so delighted to see her witness that she was prepared to overlook the poncho and its extra occupant. 'Your Honour,' she beamed, 'my witness is here.'

'So glad you could join us, Constable Fraser,'

drawled Brock. 'This trial was about to go south. You mind taking the stand?'

Politically Correct (except when it came to haranguing State Attorneys), Brock chose not to comment on the poncho and its other occupant. Siamese twins, in his book, should be treated like anyone else – even if they did have appalling taste in clothes.

'I'm not sure,' replied Benton, 'that my taking the stand would benefit the court.'

Brock leaned forwards. 'Are you pleading the fifth, son? Is that what you're doing?'

'No, Your Honour. But I don't think that my taking the stand would benefit this trial.' As Benton spoke, he inclined his head to the left in a series of peculiar, sharp movements. A twitch, thought Brock.

'I think what he's trying to say, Your Honour,' offered the other occupant of the poncho, 'is that now might be a good time for a short recess.'

'And who the hell,' barked Brock, forgetting his correctness, 'are you?'

'Detective Ray Vecchio, Chicago P.D.'

Ah, thought Brock. The name rings a bell. 'Are you two joined at the hip?' he asked, puzzled.

'In a manner of speaking, yes.' Ray, too, was beginning to develop a twitch. Everyone in the courtroom, as perplexed as the judge, looked on as the two men grimaced and jerked about inside the

155

poncho. Thatcher was at a complete loss: she was gaping, open-mouthed, at her deputy and wondering if he had finally taken a sabbatical from his senses.

'I think,' said the twitching Benton, 'that what the detective is suggesting, Your Honour, is that perhaps . . . perhaps Your Honour would feel the urge to say . . . well, I don't know . . . step out?'

Brock was now totally baffled. 'Are you telling me I have to go to the bathroom?'

Benton nodded with enthusiasm. 'Yes! That's an idea. And perhaps,' he said as he turned to the stupefied jurors, 'the members of the jury would feel the need to relieve themselves?'

One good lady, who had never attended a trial before and whose nerves had affected her bladder, raised a tentative hand.

Ray saw her. 'As a matter of fact,' he remarked to the judge, 'one does now.'

Brock was prepared to give Benton and Ray one last chance. 'Do you two,' he asked, draining his reserves of patience, 'suffer from Tourette's Syndrome?'

'Not that we're aware of,' they replied in unison, twitching again as they did so.

'Then what's with the ticks?' Brock crossed his arms on his desk and glared at the two men. 'Now, unless you want to get hit with a contempt charge, you better have a good reason why you're not sitting in that witness box right now.'

At that moment, Francis Bolt stepped into the room from behind the still-open door. 'Excuse me, but he does have a reason, Your Honour.'

Brock was now seriously annoyed. This trial was rapidly assuming the character of a farce – and not a very funny one at that. 'Who the hell,' he boomed at the sinister-looking new arrival, 'are you?'

Francis offered the judge a pious, slightly pitying look. 'A friend of Justice.'

'Right.' Brock banged his gavel on his desk. 'Exactly what the hell is going on here?'

Francis stepped forward towards Benton and Ray. 'May I remove this poncho?' Without waiting for a reply, he whipped the item over the heads of its wearers. The crowd in the courtroom, who had thus far been variously baffled, bored, amused and irritated, reacted as one: with a short, sharp scream of horror.

Underneath the poncho, Benton Fraser and Ray Vecchio were strapped to a bomb.

Once they had finished screaming, the guards reached for their weapons – only to find that the screaming interlude had wasted precious time. Two grinning men – Vern and Gabe – had already trained their own guns on them. With groans of despair, the guards obeyed their orders to let their weapons clatter to the floor.

Randall Bolt, who had until now been sitting,

grinning inanely in the dock, leaped to his feet. He let out a whoop of joy and jigged up and down a bit in front of Judge Brock. 'What's the story, Morning Glory!' he yelled in delight.

'This courtroom,' ventured his brother in an altogether more menacing voice, 'is ours.'

Randall continued jigging. Then, holding an imaginary gun in his hand, he pointed it at the judge. 'Bang, bang, Your Honour.'

'Kill me if you must,' said Brock in the sort of selfless way rarely associated with judges. 'But spare the rest of these good people.'

'Oh how kind you are.' Francis turned to the body of the room. 'Would you all like to be spared?'

No-one was sure how to react to that. They were too afraid to give the obvious answer. Knowing they were in the presence of dangerous lunatics, they feared any sort of dialogue with them. Only one person – a juror – dared reply. 'May I please,' she said as she held up a tremulous hand, 'go to the bathroom?'

'No.' Francis, like Brock before him, prided himself on the smoothness of the gatherings over which he presided. And while Brock's particular forte was the criminal trial, Francis's area of expertise was in the kidnapping, hijacking and ransom demand department. Aided, of course, by the odd bomb. 'No,' he repeated. 'Nobody is going to go anywhere for quite some time. Not until,' he added with a leer, 'we ourselves have gone.'

'And exactly how do you think you're going to get out of here?' demanded Brock, who hadn't yet got the hang of the idea that the courtroom was no longer his.

'Happily,' said Bolt, 'I have about my person a mobile phone, via which I shall now communicate my requests to the FBI.'

Oh dear, thought Ray. The FBI. If Agent Ford was going to be in charge, they would be here for ever.

An hour later, the press, the attorneys, the guards and the bailiff had been allowed to leave. The rest of the court, however, showed no sign of being permitted to adjourn. Francis Bolt had, via his handy phone, managed to make contact with the FBI and, as Ray had feared, Agent Ford had assumed control of the situation.

At least that was how Ford, rapidly responding by establishing a Situation Room in the building opposite, interpreted events. The only person in control of anything was Francis Bolt.

And Bolt was clever. Aware that his team of terrorists was, while beautifully formed, rather small, he had not attempted to take hostage the other occupants of the building. While he still held the element of surprise; while everyone was still shocked, he had instructed Vern and Gabe to usher the occupants of the other floors to safety. If the FBI needed any confirmation that his intentions were serious, that particular manoeuvre provided it. The evacuees, lest any of them be foolish enough to attempt any acts of bravery, were marched past Benton and Ray on their way outside. Vern and Gabe left them under no illusions that if they made one false move, the human bomb would be detonated. Then Francis locked the great doors of the courthouse and severed all the phone lines. Now he was totally and utterly in control.

In the building opposite, it was beginning to dawn on Ford that he was somewhat short of cards up his sleeve. Panic-stricken, and to show his team that he was masterful and in control, he paced the Situation Room, barking out questions. 'Anything?' he shouted at Agent Shorren who, in order to look busy, had been staring out of the window. Apart from an elderly lady walking a pink-rinsed poodle in the street outside, there was no activity.

'Nothing,' replied Shorren.

Ford nodded and paced again. 'What,' he snapped at the next agent, 'is the head count?'

'We have twenty in the building.' Agent Phelps, to whom Ford had addressed the same question not two minutes previously, was beginning to suspect his boss of panicking.

Ford glared at Phelps and then stopped in front of Agent McTavish. 'Communications?'

Oh for heaven's sake, thought McTavish. You know perfectly well that we can't communicate with them. 'Still nothing,' he said, remembering his imminent promotion. 'The hard lines have been severed.'

'Hmm.' Ford had run out of pacing potential. He turned to the ever-faithful Agent Deeter. 'Where are the response teams?'

'They'll be here in five.' That was probably true. The last time Ford had asked the question the answer had been six minutes. 'Right!' announced Ford to the room in general. 'Until they get here, we're going to . . .' But it was no use. Ford stalled and faltered into silence. How on earth was he supposed to know what to do if the hijackers didn't tell him what they wanted? Their unwillingness to chat was really most inconvenient.

And then the phone rang. Ford bounded over to the Situation Table and snatched the receiver. 'Ford,' he growled.

'Good Morning, Glory!' sang a happy voice at the other end. 'I need you to bring something to me.'

'They've made contact!' screamed Ford, somewhat unnecessarily.

Randall Bolt, on the other end of the line, was enjoying himself hugely. He had the entire courtroom to play in and was, as he made the call, sitting on the jury benches next to the terrified woman who, now more than ever, was desperate to go to the bathroom. Her first experience of a trial was proving rather more stressful than she had anticipated.

'And what I want you to bring me,' continued Bolt with a smile, 'is a helicopter. Do you,' he enquired politely, 'have a Bell-Star? I mean, after all, I've been kind enough to clear out most of the building for you, so the least you could do for me, I think, is get a Bell-Star on the roof within forty-five minutes. And,' he added, forestalling the outraged reply, 'if you're wondering about my destination, I'm afraid that's classified information. Oh, by the way,' he finished, 'we're sending out a little present for you in the shape of' – here Bolt adopted an excited, game-show host manner – 'Inspector Thatcher of the RCMP!' Giggling to himself, he flipped the phone shut.

On the other side of the courtroom, Gabe ushered Thatcher at gunpoint to the door. No-one noticed the concerned, near-maternal look she cast at the hapless Benton as she walked past him.

Hugely pleased with himself, Bolt leaped from the jury box and into the middle of the room to face Judge Brock. 'Before we proceed,' he announced, switching to attorney-speak, 'are there any final instructions from the bench?' At that, he roared with laughter. Brock's eyes indicated that he had thought of a good many instructions for Bolt – none of them particularly polite. His mouth, however, was unable to convey those instructions. Ten minutes previously, deciding that Brock wasn't being sufficiently deferential in 'his' courtroom, Francis had forcibly silenced the judge by taping his mouth.

'Well,' giggled his brother, 'what do you know? The bench isn't talking.' Laughing at his extraordinary wit, Bolt turned, searching for the next target for his humour. His eyes sparkled as he noticed Benton and Ray standing behind him. Both men were unusually silent, a fact largely attributable to the bomb they were wearing. Neither of them was overly familiar with the concept of being wired to an explosive – and neither relished the experience. Ray's silence, of course, was further explained by the fact that he still wasn't talking to Benton.

It was Randall's brother, however, who caught Randall's attention – and only because he demanded it. 'Randall,' he warned in a depressingly older-brother manner. 'Fifteen minutes, Randall.'

'I'll be there,' came the somewhat sulky reply.

But Francis knew his brother. 'Randall: we leave in fifteen minutes. End of sentence.'

Randall stalked up to his brother. 'Francis,' he whispered. 'I am standing here in front of a jury of my peers, for God's sake. When you use that tone of voice I hear Mom. And when I hear Mom I feel humiliated.'

'This,' hissed Francis, 'is not a point for debate, Randall. I will not have you ruin this plan the way you ruined my plan for the train. Now, you can take the spotlight your ego demands – but *I* call the shots, okay? And,' he finished with one of his nasty leers, 'I leave in fifteen minutes. With or without you – end of discussion.'

Benton and Ray were standing close enough to overhear the brothers' conversation. As they bickered, Benton leaned over and whispered into Ray's ear. 'I realize you're not talking to me,' he began, 'but I thought I'd take the liberty of posing the question anyway: why would you order a helicopter to arrive in forty-five minutes if you intend to depart in fifteen?'

Ray didn't reply.

Sighing, Benton turned his attention back to Randall Bolt, now busying himself with the courtroom camera. That camera, permanently connected to a satellite station, was about to become the mouthpiece through which he would convey his message to the outside world. Assisted by Gabe – he wasn't talking to Francis – and glad that he had worn a bandanna (very theatrical and directorly, he thought) to court, he was ready to broadcast within ten minutes.

'Wake up, America!' he boomed as the film began to roll. 'The enemy is among us!' Then, with a grandiloquent gesture towards Benton and Ray, he turned back to the camera. 'Two men stand before you, accused of treason. Their co-conspirator is no less than the American so-called Government, which daily denies the rights enshrined in our Constitution! It is time for action to be taken! Action that will teach this Government a lesson!' Then, breathing deeply in a failed-film-director sort of way, he reached his crescendo. 'The Fathers of the Confederation are sounding the alarm!'

Behind the camera, the jurors looked blankly at each other. Who the hell, their looks suggested, are the Fathers of the Confederation?

Randall Bolt noticed the bemused expressions and winced. How, he wondered, could these people possibly not know about the Fathers of The Confederation? As he glared at the jurors, one of them, evidently unaware that the members of the jury were not allowed to ask questions, raised a meek hand. 'Excuse me,' she quavered, 'but exactly who are the Fathers of the Confederation?' The question, while fearful, also carried an air of desperation. Anything, thought the lady as Randall launched into an explanation, to keep her mind off impending events in the bathroom department.

While Randall Bolt informed the world about

the nature of his cause from inside the courthouse, events outside were skipping along nicely. The media, aware of the situation, began to broadcast all manner of bulletins about it, interspersing their own footage with the live film from the courthouse. Tracey Wightman, her aubergine disguised with powder, was in her element. The siege in the courthouse had bucked her up no end coming, as it did, after her dismal encounter with the unpleasant detective. Now that her career seemed to be on the up again, she sat in the newsroom of her station, displaying elation rather than concern as she informed her viewers about the nail-biting, cliff-hanging time-bomb situation in the courtroom.

Other television presenters adopted a more sensitive approach, correctly lowering their eyes when they talked of the imprisoned jurors and the wired policemen; looking suitably stern as they recounted Randall Bolt's wayward background; appearing deeply concerned when they admitted that, as yet, they had no indication about the terrorists' demands.

But none of the broadcasts were appreciated in the Situation Room opposite the courthouse. As Agent Ford, now with a worried Thatcher at his side, watched Deeter flicking from channel to channel, his horror mounted at the ever-increasing coverage of the situation he was supposed to be resolving. 'Change it!' he snapped as the picture revealed yet another concerned anchorman. 'Change it again! Again!' But it was all to no avail: whichever channel they tuned into, the coverage was the same. Admittedly, Tracey Wightman's ghoulishly gleeful tone was original, but her content was the same.

The channel that irritated Ford most was, however, the live broadcast from the courthouse. 'Where the hell,' he asked Deeter as he watched Randall Bolt wittering on about the Fathers of the Confederation, 'is that signal coming from?'

'I don't know. I guess it must be the court TV.'

'Well, cut the signal. We're going full blackout on this one.'

Why, wondered Deeter, am I hearing voices about locking stable doors and bolting horses? Yet he wisely refrained from commenting and instead walked over to Agent McTavish, resident whizz on circuit boxes.

Ford then turned to Thatcher. 'What kind of weaponry have they got?'

'Semi-automatics. Assault rifles. Handguns.'

'How,' gasped Ford, 'did they get all that through?'

Thatcher glared at him through narrowed eyes. 'They planted one of their own on security.'

'Oh.' The word – and Thatcher was an expert on this – was uttered in a 'class dismissed' tone.

Before Thatcher could offer a scathing remark

on the inefficiency of the American security services, McTavish came running up to them. 'The circuit box,' he wailed, 'is in the building.'

Ford rounded on him. 'Then cut the cable! Blow the signal! I don't care what you do – just stop the signal.'

Charming, thought Thatcher.

'Okay, darling,' continued Ford. 'The bomb: is it real?'

It took Thatcher several seconds to register that he was again addressing her. Bristling with disapproval, she stared straight into his eyes. 'Did you just call me darling?'

Ford shrugged. 'I have no idea. Now, is the bomb real?'

'Can we afford,' she answered sweetly, 'to assume otherwise?'

Ford looked at her for a moment. She wasn't, surely, patronizing him? No, of course she wasn't. She was, after all, a woman. Suddenly Ford felt a rush of sympathy for her. Poor thing, he mused. No wonder she didn't seem capable of smiling; must be awful being in a situation like this if you're the wrong sex. To demonstrate his kindness, he patted her on the shoulder and called her a 'smart girl.'

In the courtroom, Randall Bolt had finished his potted history of the Fathers of the Confederation and was once again banging on about the necessity of sounding the alarm. 'The same alarm,' he announced to the camera and the still-baffled jurors, 'sounded on April 19th, 1775, by a simple silversmith named Paul Revere. He saddled up a horse with one thought in his mind – *the British are coming.*' Bolt lowered his voice to a reverential, admiring chant. 'All alone, he rode through the cradle of democracy. *The British are coming! The British are coming!* All alone he rode through Lexington; all alone he rode through Woburn – *The British are coming!* – He rode alone through that dark night until he finally reached Concord where he sounded his alarm . . .' Bolt placed a pretend bugle between his lips and blew on it. Then, little realizing just how much he was irritating both the jury and his viewers (particularly those who happened to be British), he warned once more that 'The British are coming!'

Benton had taken about as much as he could stand. It was one thing having a bomb wired to his chest and being tied to a man who wasn't speaking to him; quite another to be forced to listen to this inaccurate retelling of history. He turned, frowning, to Bolt. 'Objection, if I may?'

Bolt was far too stunned to reply. Wasn't he supposed to be the one in control? How could a hostage – and in particular one wired to a bomb – possibly *object*?

'Your tract,' said Benton, seizing the moment,

'contains certain inaccuracies. Paul Revere was unquestionably a patriot – but he did not make that ride alone. Nor, for that matter, did he reach Concord.'

'Oh,' sneered Bolt, aware that, as master of ceremonies, he shouldn't let some doomed Mountie upstage him. 'So you reckon he didn't, smarty pants?'

'No.' Benton was adamant. 'He didn't. Revere, a doctor named Prescott and a man named Dawes set out together from Lexington. En route, Dawes and Revere were detained by the British.'

'So who did get to Concord?' Intrigued now, Bolt forgot to sneer.

'Dr Prescott,' replied Benton, nodding to himself, 'who has been largely ignored by history, in part because of the distortions in Longfellow's poems. Distortions, I might add, that you're perpetuating in this courtroom.'

Unnoticed by Benton, Ray was staring at him in wide-eyed astonishment. Here we are, thought the policeman, held hostage in a courtroom, wired to a bomb, possibly with only minutes to live, and Benton's talking about *poetry*.

'Objection!' shouted Bolt.

But Ray overruled him by whispering urgently to Benton. 'Fraser,' he hissed, 'if you want to get us killed, why don't you just use the bombs?'

Benton looked delighted. 'I'm glad to see you're

talking to me again, Ray.'

Annoyed at the interruption, Bolt dashed up to the bench and stood beside Judge Brock. 'Does the bench sustain my objection?' he asked.

Necessarily mute because of the tape round his mouth, Brock could, he supposed, have nodded – but he wasn't going to give the madman beside him that satisfaction. Bolt, however, saw a way round that. Taking Brock's head between both hands, he nodded it vigorously back and forward. 'See?' he yelled to Benton. 'The bench does sustain!'

Benton ignored him. 'Furthermore,' he persisted, 'your assertion that he was a simple silversmith . . .'

But even Benton fell silent as the stentorian tones of Francis Bolt echoed around the room. 'Randall! Fifteen minutes.'

'Ah!' said Randall, looking towards the jurors. 'The jury will be obliged to retire to deliberate the verdict – on *them*,' he added, pointing with distaste at Benton and Ray. 'And the judge,' he sneered back at the mortified Brock, 'will be put out into the street with the rest of the trash.'

'You mean . . . you mean we can go?' stammered the bathroom lady.

'Yep,' snapped Gabe, covering them with his gun as Vern motioned for them to leave the room. 'Now get! And you,' he spat at Brock.

The assembly, minus Benton and Ray, filed out of the room. The lady with the problem, however, could only manage a hobble. And then Francis Bolt, grinning as merrily as his sepulchral appearance allowed, approached the two remaining hostages and depressed a switch on the Siamese bomb. 'Alright,' he explained, 'the heart monitors I've attached to your chests are now active. If your combined heart rate exceeds two hundred, it's bye-bye boys.' Then, delighted with his ingenuity, he tapped his forehead in a farewell salute and left the room.

Benton looked at Ray. Ray looked at Benton. Then they both looked down at the digital read-out attached to the monitors. It read 160; increased to 161 as they looked – and then rose rapidly as panic set in.

'Oh dear,' said Benton.

Chapter Eleven

The worst thing about the silence in the court-room, Ray decided, was that it was broken only by the sound of his heartbeat; his rapidly-increasing heartbeat.

Benton had already decided the same thing. Ray's heart was awfully noisy – and very fast. He took a deep breath and turned to the sweating policeman. 'Right,' he said. 'Are you nice and calm?'

Ray shrugged. Speaking to Benton was still fairly low on his agenda – and he was damned if he was going to let the other man know that he was rapidly heading towards a panic attack.

'Alright.' Benton looked down to the wires around them. 'So: we have three wires: red, white, blue. Now, if I remember correctly, it was the Continental Congress of 1872 that spelled out the meaning of the colours in the seal. Red was meant to stand for heartiness and courage; white was meant to stand for purity and innocence, and blue was meant to stand for vigilance and justice – all of which no terrorist would object to. So,' he finished with a smile, 'where does that leave us?'

Ray rolled his eyes. 'In the middle of a courtroom, strapped to a bomb, waiting to blow up. Where the hell do you think it leaves us?'

'Ray, Ray, don't get excited . . .'

'Look, we are going to die! You want me to pretend I'm happy about it?'

'Ray, if you're bitten by a rattlesnake, the safest course of action is to lower your metabolic rate.'

'This,' screamed Ray, 'is not a rattlesnake! This is a plastic explosive!'

Benton didn't disagree. 'But, the same principle would apply . . .'

'You really should listen to yourself sometimes. You sound like a robot.'

Benton thought the remark extremely unkind but, under the circumstances, was prepared to overlook it. The circumstances had anyway crept up beyond 170. 'Ray,' he said, making a soothing gesture with his arm. 'Just calm down.'

'Don't tell me to calm down, okay? I'm looking at Judgement Day here. Don't tell me to calm down!'

'Ray . . . if we just work together . . .'

'Can you honestly say that you are calm right now?'

'No,' admitted Benton. 'I'm . . . Well, I'm . . .'

'What?'

Benton paused, searching for the right word. 'Concerned,' he said at length.

'Concerned?' squeaked Ray. 'That's it? You don't feel anger? You're not angry?'

'No. Not exactly, not . . .'

'God!' sighed Ray. 'Will you just admit that you're a human being? Just once in your life, can you admit . . .'

'Please.' Benton was looking at the read-out. '*Please*, Ray . . .'

'. . . that you're a human being?'

As Ray spoke, the reading reached 199 and Benton, in a last-ditch attempt to save their lives, threw himself into a trance. His head fell forward on to his chest and he emitted a distinctly unhuman noise that sounded, to his surprised companion, like 'om'.

'What on earth are you doing?'

'Dropping my heart-rate,' mumbled Benton.

'In the middle of an argument!'

'Don't let me stop you,' shrugged Benton as he relaxed further and the reading began to descend.

'I'm going to kill you,' snarled Ray.

'Yes,' nodded Benton. 'That's very possible.' Teetering on the cusp of a coma, Benton was the epitome of calm. Yet knowing that he should try to placate his friend, he surprised him by adding, 'I've never hated you, Ray. I've envied you, maybe . . .'

'Envied me?' Ray's heart missed a beat – a good omen in the monitor department. He looked round, astounded, at the near-somnolent Benton.

His eyes were closed, but his next words showed him to be perfectly lucid.

'I'm not proud of it, Ray, but you have a kind of freedom I wish I had. A sort of existential honesty.'

'You're saying I'm honest?' What an extraordinary thing, thought Ray, to say to a cop.

'In your heart? Yes.'

Ray could only stare in shocked admiration; an admiration tinged with a warm glow of affection that served to lower the read-out even further.

In the Situation Room, the situation was not good. But at least Ford had something new to talk about: the Rapid Response Team, having been delayed by a flat tyre and a pit-stop for bagels, had arrived. He debriefed them at length, informing them all about the Bolt brothers, the history of the Fathers of the Confederation and, for good measure, a smattering of the stirring story of Paul Revere's ride. He left out any mention of distortions to the latter by the poet Longfellow.

But the most interesting part of his debrief, as far as the jurors would have been concerned had they been present, was that he included them in the hostage-count. And this, despite the fact that they had been released from the courtroom fifteen minutes previously. What, they would have wondered (had they been there) had happened to them?

Sidelined by the simmering testosterone,

Thatcher had been shuffled to the corner of the room. She stood, quietly contemplating Ford's murder, as she watched him gesticulate towards the courtroom. Then, as often happens when the action needs to rip along a little faster, she had an idea. Turning to the Records Clerk squeezed into the corner of the room (the clerk was also female), she asked if she would be kind enough to find a list of all the trials scheduled for the court that day.

Five minutes later, as Ford was outlining grandiose plans for an armed assault of the courthouse, the clerk returned with the requested file. 'Courtroom one,' she read to Thatcher, 'an ongoing manslaughter. Court two – a fraud, first day. Three – a series of misdemeanours . . .'

'Hold it.' Thatcher leaned forward. 'What was the fraud?'

'Er . . . hang on. The details are on the next page . . . oh, here.' With the sort of smile that Ford dismissed as feminine, she handed the sheet of paper to Thatcher.

On the other side of the room, Ford was becoming distinctly hot under the collar as his plans unfolded in his mind. 'The Red Team,' he shouted, 'will lead at staging area B; the chopper will lift off at thirteen hundred hours . . . rooftop E.T.A. is thirteen-o-five. The Blue Team,' he continued, prodding the Situation Drawing on the Situation Table, 'will be in readiness at staging area A. White team will be in like readiness at staging area C. On my go,' he finished, 'we move. Any questions?'

The men in front of him were far too bamboozled even to open their mouths. Thatcher, however, was not. She charged across the room and stomped to an antagonistic halt in front of the senior agent. 'Yes. Excuse me can I see you . . .' Without giving Ford a chance to object, she manhandled him across the room. 'I know this man Bolt,' she hissed. 'He won't leave things to chance.' She gestured dismissively at the Situation Drawing and its acolytes. 'He'll have anticipated all this. If you . . .'

'Yeah.' Ford stalled her with a patronizing sneer. 'I appreciate your thoughts, darling. I really do. But,' he cautioned, wagging a finger, 'let's get something straight: this isn't a train. You're on my turf now.' Then he turned on his heel and rejoined the testosterone.

'He called me "darling" again?' mouthed Thatcher, gibbering with rage and disbelief. 'He called me "darling".' Suddenly she felt depressed. She would get over the darling business – but how would she ever get her point across to Ford about the other matter, the fraud trial? For Thatcher now knew what Ford did not: the trial had revolved round thirty million dollars worth of bearer bonds. And those bonds were locked in the safe of the courthouse. It didn't require the biggest brain on earth (so Ford's grey cells were well out of the running) to deduce that the calculating, clinical Francis Bolt was after those bonds.

'Fraser, wake up.'

Responding with spooky alacrity, Benton raised his head, opened his eyes and looked at Ray. 'Are you calm?'

'Yes,' sighed Ray. 'I'm calm.'

'Are you sure you're calm?'

'I said,' grunted Ray through gritted teeth, 'I'm calm. Now don't get me aggravated.'

Benton registered the higher pitch of Ray's voice, the prelude to agitation. 'Alright,' he soothed. 'Alright, alright.'

'What,' said Ray suddenly, 'was blue again?'

'Blue stood for vigilance and justice.'

Ray looked pensive. 'Justice,' he repeated. 'Justice . . . we're in a justice building.'

Benton stiffened. Eyes shining, he turned to Ray. 'That's it!'

'Benny, calm down!'

'No, no, no!' Benton was almost feverish with excitement. 'You got it!'

'I said,' warned Ray as he looked at the digital counter, 'calm down!'

'But Ray . . . !'

'Calm Down!' Ray had trouble keeping his voice steady as he saw the reading hit 199.

Benton saw it too. 'Oh dear,' he said. Then,

emitting a gentle 'om' he slumped forward – but not as quickly as Ray. 'Omming' quietly, he had already snapped into trance position.

Ray broke the silence when the reading dropped below seventy. 'Are you calm?' he enquired.

'Yes.' Benton took a deep breath and, referring back to the source of his excitement, gestured to the wires around their chests. 'So . . . it's blue?'

'Yeah. Blue. Maybe.'

'Okay, well, let's go with blue.'

'No!' Ray was not happy with the lingering element of doubt. '*You* go with blue.'

Benton seemed peeved. 'Why don't you go with blue?'

'Well,' shrugged Ray, ''cos you're better at this.'

'Maybe,' suggested Benton, 'we should both go with blue.' He looked round and locked eyes with Ray.

Realizing that their options were somewhat limited, Ray nodded. As one, they reached for the wire that, if Benton was right, represented vigilance and justice. Involuntarily closing their eyes, they pulled it away from the bomb mechanism. Their vigilance paid off: there was no explosion; no noise apart from a tiny click as the digital counter shut off. They had defused the bomb. They were still alive.

Now that he had been given back the gift of life, Ray felt like a child suddenly thrown into the outside world. 'What,' he asked in tones of wonder, 'do we do now?'

'We go and find the terrorists. Then we foil them.'

Suddenly Ray remembered why he had sent his friend to Coventry. Wouldn't any normal person, any human being, just want to get the hell out of the building? Run to safety? But no, Benton wanted to rush up to the roof to grapple with terrorists. 'Fraser . . .'

But it was no use: Benton was already at the other end of the courtroom, hauling open the heavy double doors. 'The roof, Ray,' he explained as if Ray didn't already know. 'We must get to the roof.' With that, he shot out into the foyer. Sighing in exasperation, Ray followed him.

They stopped in their tracks as they took in the macabre sight that greeted them in front of the lift shaft. One of the jurors (she who had so sorely sought relief) was standing between the two lift doors. Her mouth was gagged, her body draped in a toga-like sheet, and in her outstretched left hand she was holding a set of scales. There was a crown on her head; one that wouldn't win prizes in the style wars but that nevertheless broadcast an extremely clear message. It was made of explosives.

Behind Benton, Ray gasped. 'What . . . ?'

'A parody of "Justice", Ray.'

'I know that!'

The lady, rigid with fear, turned her pleading eyes on the two men.

Benton sprang forward. 'Ma'am,' he urged, 'just try to remain calm.'

'Fraser!'

'I can't help her, Ray,' whispered Benton. 'Look at those.'

Ray looked. On either side of the terrified woman was a mound of explosives. They were wired to the object that, under happier circumstances, might have been a clutch bag clasped to her waist. Except this clutch bag was, in fact, a detonator. And there were other wires leading off the detonator, heading upwards to the next floor.

Benton looked at the lift panel. The indicators told him that both lifts were on the roof. 'The stairs!' he yelled to Ray. Then, as he turned towards the stairwell door, he sought to alleviate the unhappy woman's distress. 'Be right back,' he smiled. Somewhat unnecessarily, he added 'Don't move.'

Both men thundered up the stairs and burst into the foyer of the first floor. The sight that greeted them beside the lifts was exactly the same – apart from the fact that 'Justice' was a man. The next floor was the same – and the next. 'There are twelve floors in the building,' panted Ray as they ran upwards, 'and twelve members of the jury.'

'Yes. They've stationed one on every floor and it's my guess they're linked to the same detonator frequency.'

'So when they blow,' said Ray with a shudder, 'the whole building blows.' So why, he wondered to himself, am I climbing upwards instead of getting the hell out of here? He refused to let himself believe that it was anything to do with jealousy of Benton; declined to listen to the little voice in his head telling him that there was no way he could let Benton steal all the glory – again.

Escaping through the front doors of the courtroom would anyway have been impossible: the Bolt brothers and their 'cousins' had returned to the ground floor via the service stairwell. They were accompanied by a somewhat reluctant third party.

Francis Bolt's passion for accuracy and neat mathematical formulas meant that Judge Brock was out of luck in the parody of 'Justice' department. With, as Ray had said, twelve floors and twelve jurors, there was no place for him in that particular scheme.

'But worry not!' as Francis had said to Brock, lest he feel upset at being left out. He had other, equally dramatic plans for the judge.

They involved another telephone call to Agent Ford across the road: a call that he made mere seconds before Ford sent the Rapid Response Team into the courthouse. A call that stopped Ford in his tracks.

'Agent Ford?' purred Francis into his mobile as the call was answered. 'Before you send in that Rapid Response Team which you have no doubt been readying, why don't you take a gander at the front doors of the courthouse?'

Ford hesitated. What to do? Ignore the madman and send in the troops anyway? Then he looked up at the rest of the testosterone team. They had all heard Bolt on the Situation Room's speaker-phone and now they were rushing, to a man (and two women) to the window. Furious, terrified he was losing control, Ford followed them.

As they stood, looking down at the courthouse door, Bolt's voice again wafted through the speaker-phone. 'I have it on good authority,' he boasted, 'that our judge is an avid fan of the death penalty. So,' he added with a chuckle, 'I think he should lead by example, don't you?'

The occupants of the Situation Room exchanged perplexed looks. What the hell was Bolt on about? Nothing was happening at the courthouse door. But as they looked down again, something did happen – something even more macabre than the sights witnessed by Benton and Ray.

Judge Brock, strapped into a customized electric chair (it had been fitted with castors), shot through the revolving doors of the courthouse. As if fired by a cannon, he barrelled across the pavement, clattered off the kerb and shuddered to an uneasy stop in the middle of the deserted street.

'Good God!' exclaimed Deeter. 'What on earth . . .?'

'Oh,' interrupted Bolt from the speaker-phone. 'It was a sad day in Illinois when the State opted for that lethal injection. You know,' he added, 'call me old-fashioned if you like, but I think there's something . . . I don't know . . . something elegant about the electric chair.'

Judge Brock would have disagreed. Still gagged, totally unable to move, he looked down at the contraption in his lap. A variation of the 'Justice' clutch-bag, its wires protruded upwards, terminating at the strange skull-cap he was wearing. Brock had been around long enough to know he was wired to a bomb. Yet as he sat in the middle of the street, he saw the television cameras behind the distant cordon being trained on him. The bomb he could come to terms with: the humiliation, however, was insufferable. I must, he groaned to himself, look so *stupid*.

'He looks,' said Ford as he looked, 'so . . .'

'Look closely,' interrupted Bolt again, 'and you'll see that our man is wired.'

'Yep,' said Deeter, brandishing binoculars. 'He's for real.'

Suddenly all was quiet in the Situation Room as the New Situation sank in. It was Bolt, still on the phone, who broke the silence. 'You have fourteen minutes,' he warned, 'to get me that chopper. If you fail, first I do the judge and then I do the jury.'

Ford knew when he was beaten. Shoulders slumped in defeat, he turned to the body of the room. 'Response Team,' he groaned. 'Stand down.'

Beside him, Thatcher remained expressionless. Yet behind her mask, where there might have been sadness, there was a faint glimmer of hope. Benton was still in there, and where there was Benton there was the Mountie who always got his man.

Chapter Twelve

Ray and Benton raced out on to the courthouse roof. Now that Ray was rather keen on the idea of tackling the terrorists instead of running away from them, he was miffed to find the roof deserted. He demonstrated his annoyance by emitting a petulant wail as he looked around. 'Where the hell,' he pouted, 'have they got to? They should be here.'

'Unless,' replied a frowning Benton, 'the helicopter was a diversion.'

'What do you . . .?'

But Benton, thinking ahead, had already rushed to the edge of the roof and was looking down at the street below. The sight of the bound and gagged judge confirmed the suspicions that had been forming in his mind: for reasons of their own (terrorists always had selfish motives), Bolt and his cronies had returned to the ground floor.

Then, scanning upwards, Benton saw Thatcher standing at a window in the building opposite. So, now beside him, did Ray. 'Hey!' began the latter. 'Isn't that . . .'

'Yes. Your people must have established a situation room to monitor the courthouse.'

'Not my people,' snorted Ray, recognizing the busy-looking person standing beside Thatcher. 'The FBI.'

'Mmm. Shame. Anyway,' mused Benton, 'we shall have to endeavour to exchange information with them.'

'And exactly how are we supposed to do that? By semaphore?' Benny, thought Ray, really does come up with the most fatuous notions. Exchange information indeed.

'Yes,' replied Benton. 'By semaphore.' Then he further startled Ray by thrusting a bag at him. 'Hold this, will you?'

Ray peered into the bag. 'Why are we carrying our own bomb around with us?'

'It might come in handy.' Without further ado, Benton stepped forward on to the edge of the roof and started signalling with his arms.

In the Situation Room opposite, Ford let out a sharp, derisive laugh at the sight of the flapping Mountie. 'Ha! What does he reckon he's doing? Trying to communicate by semaphore?'

'Yes,' snapped Thatcher, moving as close to the glass as she could get. Then she too started flapping.

Their silent method of conversation looked ridiculous – but it worked.

'What is the status,' signalled Benton, 'of the Response Team?'

'Standing down,' flapped Thatcher.

'Good. Do not activate. The jury is linked to explosives.'

Oh dear, thought Thatcher. 'Where,' she waved, 'are the terrorists?'

'I have no idea. Do you?'

If I did, thought Thatcher, I wouldn't be asking the question, now would I? Suddenly Benton was, in her mind, just another man; another brainless member of the testosterone team. 'I'm not,' she gesticulated, 'the one who's in the building, am I?' For good measure, she added the suffix 'moron'.

On the courthouse roof and piqued at being left out of a conversation which, judging by Thatcher's expression, was becoming somewhat heated, Ray leaned towards Benton. 'What did she say?'

Benton turned, bristling with indignation. 'She called me a moron.'

Ray was impressed. 'That is one very perceptive woman.'

Looking back at Thatcher, Benton made a request that she would no doubt consider moronic but that, to him, was of the utmost importance. 'Could you,' he asked, 'have someone retrieve Diefenbaker?'

To his surprise, Thatcher signalled a 'yes'. Then she broached the subject that Ford had dismissed without even considering: the fraud trial. She semaphored for Benton to ask Ray about it. An error in communication, however, meant that her request translated as 'ask Ray about Gambello cheese' instead of 'the Gambello case'. Under the impression that Thatcher was making her own domestic request in response to the Diefenbaker agreement, Benton agreed.

'What,' he asked as he turned to Ray, 'is Gambello cheese like?'

'Gambello cheese? Never heard of it . . . Look! Good God! Thatcher's just punched Ford in the face.'

She had indeed. The FBI agent, annoyed and deeply suspicious about the semaphoring performance, had barked a 'Look darlin', I need to know what you're telling him.' Eyes glinting, Thatcher saw the opportunity she had been waiting for. Seizing the moment and, under the guise of a particularly vigorous piece of semaphoring, she had walloped him in the face. Then, without breaking stride or even looking round, she continued communicating with Benton.

Benton turned back to the Situation Window to see Ford sprawling on the ground as Thatcher signalled 'Spelling mistake. I meant "the Gambello case". And,' she added as a *quid pro quo* for the Diefenbaker Agreement, 'pick up coffee on return to the Consulate.'

'Understood,' responded Benton. With a final flap, he signalled 'end communication.' Then he turned to the baffled Ray. 'Ray, tell me about the Gambello case.'

'Ah. Got you now. Big-scale fraud,' said Ray with a frown. 'Thirty million in U.S. bearer bonds. Like cash in hand. The bonds,' he added, 'are part of the evidence in the trial and the trial, funnily enough, is . . . Oh!'

'Exactly,' said Benton with a grim smile. 'The trial was scheduled for today, which means those bonds are in this building.'

'So the helicopter *was* a diversion,' replied a wide-eyed Ray. 'They're going to grab the bonds and head . . . well, where?' As he pondered their exit route, he swung Benton's bag to and fro – an unwise move, considering its contents.

Benton grabbed the bomb back and headed towards the stairwell. 'I reckon they'll head for the sewers. Then,' he added, quickening his pace as he remembered the jurors, 'they'll detonate from a safe distance.'

Escaping by way of the sewers was indeed part of Francis Bolt's masterplan. But first he had to execute the other, more pleasurable parts.

One of them, as Benton and Ray left the roof, was already nearing completion. In the evidence room of the courthouse, Vern and Gabe had just succeeded in breaking into the safe containing the bearer bonds. Francis, standing behind them with his brother, was delighted. As the massive steel door swung open, he patted Vern on the back. 'Thank you, cousin,' he said with as warm a smile as he could muster. 'Your reward is nigh.'

Nigh came quickly to Vern. And to Gabe. As soon as the four men had finished loading the bearer bonds into the athletic bag that had originally contained Benton, the Bolt brothers swung into action, belting their cousins across the head and knocking them to the ground. Then they set to work on the binding and gagging at which they had recently had so much practice. 'Sorry about that, cousins,' grinned Francis as the brothers took their leave. 'It just makes the maths easier.' A pity, he mused as they left the evidence room, that the family had to break up in such an unfortunate way, but dividing thirty million dollars by four would leave the sort of messy, unpleasing number that he simply couldn't abide. 'Long division,' he said to his brother as they clattered down the stairs towards the basement, 'is such a pain.'

Above them, Benton and Ray found themselves with a problem. The Bolts had jammed the lifts, precluding a swift descent into the bowels of the building. The doors from the hallway were open – but instead of leading into the lift cars they gave on to the deep, dark shafts.

'Oh well,' shrugged Ray, recoiling in distaste from the abyss. 'we'll just have to leg it down the stairs.'

'Unless . . .' mused Benton, reaching for the lift cables dangling in front of them.

'No!'

'It's easy, Ray. Just pretend you're a fireman.'

'I never wanted to be a fireman! I only ever wanted to be a policeman!'

'Ray, Ray, Ray. Stay calm.'

'I am calm!'

'Look.' Benton lunged forward, wrapped his legs round the cable and, dangling in mid-air, grinned back at Ray. 'See. It's easy.'

'It's dangerous, Benton.'

'Ray,' sighed his friend. 'We are in a courtroom wired with explosives and unless we move quickly we will die.'

'Well, since you put it that way . . .' Ray closed his eyes and leaped into the darkness. 'Hey!' he exclaimed as he clung on to the cable adjacent to Benton's and began to shin downwards. 'This is easy!'

Benton grinned and, in tandem with Ray, began the swift descent. 'Uh-oh,' he said after a moment.

'What?'

'Oh . . . it's nothing. Just a little friction.' Benton didn't want to alarm Ray, but his gloved left hand was beginning to smoulder against the metal cable. He tried to ignore the unpleasantly warm sensation and looking down, concentrated on the job in hand. Then his glove burst into flames, and not even he could ignore the fact that disaster was imminent. 'Oh dear,' he said.

'What?'

'Well, it would appear . . . it would seem that . . . yep, I'm on fire, Ray.'

'Oh well, at least the whole day isn't a total write-off.' But Ray regretted the remark almost as soon as he had said it: Benton fell off the cable and, human fireball, plunged downwards. Ray felt a twinge of reluctant admiration for the friend he was about to lose. How, he wondered, can a man on fire and hurtling towards death not even scrcam?

Benton didn't die. The fire, however, proved to have a very short life-span. With a splash and a sad little hiss, it extinguished itself in the puddle of water at the bottom of the shaft – the same puddle that saved Benton.

Ray was overjoyed when he joined Benton by more orthodox means. 'Well,' he panted, indicating the puddle. 'That was lucky.'

'Well, not luck, exactly,' corrected Benton. There's usually a puddle at the bottom of an elevator . . .'

'No there isn't.'

Benton didn't want to sound preachy, but facts were, after all, facts. 'Well, as a rule, yes, actually, there is. You see,' he began, 'the condensation . . .'

'Shut up!'

Benton shut up.

'We are now,' said Ray, anxious to take the lead

in a different subject, 'in the basement. If we're right about the terrorists, then they'll be here as well, so we'd better be careful. Any sound . . . hey! What's that?'

Benton cocked an ear. 'A sound?'

'I know it's a sound!' gibbered Ray. 'But what sort of sound? It sounds like . . .'

'A whine?'

'Don't be ridiculous. Terrorists don't whine.'

But wolves whine. Comprehension dawning on both men at the same time, they looked up to where, twelve feet above them, the lift shaft joined the basement. There, tail wagging and whining excitedly, stood an ecstatic Diefenbaker.

Dief's arrival on the scene was not attributable to a contrived literary device. It was, in fact, perfectly rational and easily explained. In the Situation Room, with a dearth of activity buzzing around her, Thatcher had been able to phone the Consulate as soon as the semaphoring episode was over. Constable Cooper, holding the fort and polishing his coffee-making routine, had taken the call and had immediately ventured forth to release the wolf from his incarceration in Benton's flat. After that, Diefenbaker had taken control. He had dragged the hapless Cooper across Chicago by his lead and, with the sixth sense that had thus far eluded Benton's father (who had anyway departed on holiday with Frobisher), had led him to the underground garage that led directly to the courtroom. Unfortunately for Cooper, the entrance to the garage had been wolf-sized rather than human, and Cooper had been obliged to part company with Diefenbaker. He was, as Dief reached Benton and Ray, in the process of nursing his wounds – an activity with which Agent Ford could identify. Ford was skulking in the Situation Room, distancing himself as far as he could from Thatcher and nursing the bloody nose she had inflicted on him with her energetic semaphoring.

But the two men in the lift shaft had no thought for Ford, Cooper or even Thatcher. Diefenbaker's arrival on the scene injected new energy and new hope into their mission and, mere seconds after his appearance, they had climbed out of the shaft and were once more on the hunt for the villains.

They didn't have to hunt very far: Francis and Randall Bolt were, as Ray had surmised, making sounds in the control room of the courthouse basement: sounds not unrelated to their endeavours to pull the manhole cover off the entrance to the sewers.

The two men and the wolf, lurking by the door of that room, watched them in silence. Thinking like a policeman (not surprising, given his line of work), Ray reached down to his ankle holster and extracted his gun – something he had been itching to do for ages.

Benton, however, was thinking about using a different and altogether more surprising weapon – Diefenbaker. 'Go!' he urged the wolf as he pointed to the terrorists.

Dief moved swiftly, and to great effect. He pelted into the control room and, before the Bolt brothers could even register what had happened, relieved them of the athletic bag containing the bearer bonds. Then the trio ran hell-for-leather through the basement towards freedom.

Freedom, however, played hard to get: they came horribly unstuck in the fan circulation room at the far end of the basement – mainly because that room was, if rooms can be such, a cul-de-sac.

'Oh dear,' said Benton as they took in the situation. 'I think . . .'

'Gentlemen!' boomed a voice from the doorway. 'You have one choice: you can give us what we want or we blow the building.' Ray, Benton and Diefenbaker scrambled for cover behind an air-conditioning unit. Then Ray surprised the life out of Benton by yelling back at Randall Bolt. 'You are not going to blow the building,' he shouted. 'You are not a martyr. You're just a self-centred little creep who wants to get his face in the paper.'

'Ray!' Benton looked round, deeply wounded, at his friend. 'You're not talking about me, are you?'

'Indirectly.'

'You're wrong about this,' bellowed Bolt from

the doorway. 'I'm on a midnight ride for America! I am a modern version of . . . of . . . what was that guy's name again?'

'Dr Prescott,' obliged Benton.

'That's right. I'm the modern version of Dr Prescott.'

Randall's brother, however, begged to differ. 'No you're not,' he snapped indignantly. 'You're *not*, Randall. And neither am I.'

Randall turned to his brother in astonishment. 'What on earth are you saying?'

'See the world for what it is, Randall. We are not patriots. We are thieves. Uncommon – but thieves nonetheless. And once again,' he finished with a weary sigh, 'you are on the verge of ruining a perfect plan.'

Behind the air-conditioning unit, Benton turned to Ray. 'We seem to have hit a nerve, Ray.'

'Detective!' shouted Francis, opting to address the current situation and reserve the filial argument for a more convenient time. 'There are twelve innocent people in jeopardy. Is it worth the risk? All we want are the bonds.'

Ray could hardly believe his ears. 'Are you kidding me?' he yelled back. 'That,' he added to Benton, 'is all they want? Why on earth didn't they say so in the first place?' Reaching behind him, he grabbed the athletic bag and hurled it down the length of the room. 'Take them!' he yelled to the Bolts.

'Ray!' Benton was outraged. 'For God's sake, what are you doing? That's not ours.'

'I know. It's theirs.'

'It is not theirs,' insisted Benton. 'That money belonged to someone else.'

'Oh.' Comprehension dawning, Ray looked at the other athletic bag – the one that Diefenbaker had filched from the Bolts. 'Did they say "bonds"? I thought they said "bombs".'

Benton thought – temporarily forgetting that Ray was American – that his friend was being modest. 'That's very clever, Ray,' he said in admiration.

'Yes,' said Ray, capitalizing on Benton's misunderstanding, 'it was, wasn't it?'

The Bolts, however, weren't so clever. Relieved to have retrieved what they thought was the bag of bonds, they scampered through the basement towards the sewer manhole and safety, quite forgetting that there was an obstacle between them and safety: the lift shaft.

Disaster was made complete by the fact that Randall dropped the detonator on the edge of the shaft as he fell, screaming, into the puddle that had saved Benton.

Half an hour later a media circus had descended on the courthouse. Tracey Wightman and Agent Ford, both sporting red noses, provided the clown element. The jurors, carrying their "Justice" outfits, provided the drama. The scrum of civilians provided a shrieking audience and Judge Brock, happily released from his electric chair, presided over the proceedings with the air of gravitas he felt was sorely needed. He had quite forgotten he was still wearing his crown of explosives.

But every circus needs a star – and that star was Diefenbaker. Here, thought the scrum of journalists and broadcasters, was a true hero. Forgotten was the irritatingly modest Mountie, the self-effacing law-enforcer who, they now acknowledged to themselves, had never been worthy of their attention. He had even lacked the basic ingredient of heroism: American nationality.

The fact that Diefenbaker, too, was Canadian didn't bother them. He possessed a quality so special that it transcended any minor faults: a quality essential to stardom.

That quality was a studied nonchalance; a seeming (though calculated) indifference to the attention surrounding him. He sat outside the courthouse, assuming a bored, hugely photogenic air of insouciance. And he consolidated his star status by steadfastly refusing to say a word.

Benton and Ray were nowhere in sight – largely because they were back on the roof. Benton, to his consternation, had left his hat on the ledge.

It was from that ledge, high above the media circus, that they watched Diefenbaker.

'Press hound,' said Ray in amused admiration.

Benton turned and smiled at his friend. 'Who needs it?'

Ray grinned back. 'Not us.'

'Nope. Not us.'

Feeling suddenly expansive, Ray stretched his arms out, embracing the panorama before them. 'God!' he exclaimed. 'I love this city. You know,' he added, nodding to himself. 'Sometimes you have to be a conduit. Sometimes you have to let the world come to you. You know what I'm saying?'

'Sure,' said Benton, accepting the tacit apology; delighted that they were firm friends again. Smiling, feeling happy with the world, he looked down again at the scrum below them. As he surveyed the circus, a figure in red detached itself from the main body of the crowd and looked up at him. Then it started flapping its arms around.

'You have duties, Constable,' it signalled.

Benton flapped back a dutiful 'understood'. Then, unable to help himself, he added words that brought a bashful smile to the face twelve floors below: 'Red suits you'.

Ray's eyes narrowed as he watched the semaphoring couple. 'What,' he demanded when Benton had finished, 'was all that about?'

'What? Oh,' shrugged Benton, emulating Diefenbaker's nonchalance, 'that.'

'Yes. That.'

'Oh. Nothing.'

'Nothing? You're standing there flailing your arms around like you're daffy? What do you think? I just got off the boat or something?'

'Which boat?'

'Do not,' snarled Ray, 'try to deflect this . . .'

'Deflect what?'

'You know what I'm talking about.'

'Well, no, Ray. I don't know what you're talking about.'

Ray began to flail his arms around, unconsciously semaphoring his mounting rage. 'After all we've been through: haven't you learned *anything*?'

Benton frowned. 'In what sense?'

Ray exhaled in exasperation and glared at the other man. 'You are the most irritating man in the world.'

Benton paused before replying; a reply that sent Ray storming towards the stairwell entrance. 'Define irritating.'

'No,' snorted Ray over his shoulder. 'You look it up, Mr Encyclopedia.'

Benton wrinkled his nose. He didn't want to sound patronizing, but . . . 'I think,' he said as he followed Ray, 'that you mean Mr Dictionary, don't you?'

But Ray had already disappeared into the building, stomping down the stairs and swearing that he would never, *ever* talk to Benton again.